Dear Reader,

I am so incredibly excited to welcome you to the action-packed world of Team Chu! This series is going to be one wild ride, featuring Clip and Sadie Chu, two of the most competitive siblings you will ever meet!

Join them on the first of many adventures in *Team Chu and the Battle of Blackwood Arena*, in which they encounter a sinister game of laser tag that might be trying to trap them forever. The Chus must bring all their speed, smarts, and strategy if they want to escape . . . and maybe even learn to work together along the way. Luckily, they've got a hilarious group of friends to help them face the dangerous virtual battlegrounds, including the Haunted Castle, the Abandoned Space Station, and the Mad Scientist's Lab!

Middle grade books are quite possibly my favorite to read and write, and stories in this age category got me started on the path to becoming an author! I love that they can be zany and fun, and at the same time, deal with all the ups and downs of middle school life.

Team Chu and the Battle of Blackwood Arena brings together so many different elements of my own life, from the '90s Nickelodeon shows I used to watch as a kid (like

Guts and *Legends of the Hidden Temple*) to the competitiveness between siblings (I have two younger brothers, and we still battle it out on video games and in escape rooms to this day!).

I had such a blast writing this book, and I genuinely hope that you will have just as much fun reading it.

Now, gear up 'cause it's game time!

See you in the arena,

JULIE

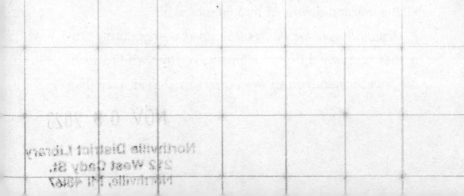

TEAM CHU
AND THE BATTLE OF BLACKWOOD ARENA

A Team Chu Adventure

TEAM CHU
AND THE BATTLE OF
BLACKWOOD ARENA

JULIE C. DAO

SQUARE
FISH

FARRAR STRAUS GIROUX
NEW YORK

SQUARE FISH

An imprint of Macmillan Publishing Group, LLC
120 Broadway, New York, NY 10271 • mackids.com

Our books may be purchased in bulk for promotional, educational, or
business use. Please contact your local bookseller or the Macmillan
Corporate and Premium Sales Department at (800) 221-7945 ext. 5442
or by email at MacmillanSpecialMarkets@macmillan.com.

Library of Congress Cataloging-in-Publication Data is available.

Originally published in the United States by Farrar Straus Giroux
First Square Fish edition, 2023
Book designed by Trisha Previte
Square Fish logo designed by Filomena Tuosto
Printed in the United States of America by Lakeside Book Company,
Harrisonburg, Virginia

ISBN 978-1-250-80545-4
10 9 8 7 6 5 4 3 2 1

TO JON AND JUSTIN:

Proud to be on Team Dao with you!

CHAPTER ONE
SADIE

FIGURES CLOSE IN ON ME IN THE DARK.

I crouch against the padded wall, making myself as small as possible. The music blares, and the heavy bass pounds along with my heart. My helmet feels too tight over my ponytail, but there's no time to fix it. I raise my phaser, finger on the red button, and peer around the corner. I can't see anyone, but I know my teammates are hiding, covering me from behind.

There's a flash of movement.

Someone was clueless enough to wear a white T-shirt into the arena. I shake my head, watching it glow in the black lights. They might as well have worn a target on their back. Shouts ring out, and red laser beams slice through the darkness.

Time to make my move.

I run with my shoulders hunched, protecting the "strike zones" on my chest and waist, and skirt the area where White Shirt's getting ambushed. If an enemy laser hits me one more time, I'm out of the game, and I can't let my team down. We've made it this far across the arena.

"Sadie!" someone hisses in my ear. I whirl to see my best friend, Jeremy Thomas, whose helmet barely fits over his curly cloud of hair. He yanks me into an alcove formed by two padded mats. "I lost Iggy back there. I don't know where he is."

I say a bad word that my brother taught me. "So it's just you and me?"

Jeremy's teeth are ultra white against his dark skin. "It's just you and me."

The electronic dance music booms harder than ever. Ten feet away, the roaming strobe lights illuminate our goal: a swinging rope ladder leading to a tower. The tower means safety. The tower means victory. The tower means *bragging rights*.

I grin, imagining Clip's face when he sees that his eleven-year-old sister has crushed him at his own game. "Okay. Here's what we're gonna do," I tell Jeremy, in a low, businesslike voice. "You hold both our phasers and get on my back. That'll protect you. I'll carry you to the ladder, and then you climb up. Don't look back."

Jeremy looks doubtfully from his chubby frame to my scrawny one. "Are you sure? I just had, like, a gallon of fries, and my dad always says salt makes your body hold water."

"And my grandpa says I'm strong for my size, like an ant. I can carry you," I say confidently. "I *will* carry you."

His eyes mist over. "This is just like Sam and Frodo going up Mount Doom."

Shouts break out not far from us. If that is Clip's team, then their distraction is the window we need. I bend over so Jeremy can clamber onto my back. "No matter what you see or hear, you keep climbing that ladder and get yourself up to the tower. Okay?" I ask.

"But what about you?"

"Don't worry about me. *You're* the President, and once I get you to safety, we win. Doesn't matter if the enemy takes me down."

Jeremy grips my shoulder solemnly. "You're a hero, Sadie Chu."

I give him my phaser and grab his legs behind the knees. "Victory, here we come," I whisper, and then I run at full throttle toward the rope ladder.

It happens so fast, I'm on the ground before I know it. Figures burst from the shadows and tackle us, sending Jeremy to the ground with a yelp. The sudden loss of

balance pulls me onto my back on the padded floor mat. The edge of my helmet presses into my skull as I stare up at my older brother's smug face. He aims his phaser right at the target on my chest.

"Any last words, Chu?" he asks.

"It ain't over yet, Chu," I bite out, scrambling for my phaser before I remember that I gave it to Jeremy. I groan as Clip smirks and pushes his button. A red laser beam emerges and hits the strike zone on my vest with a high-pitched *ping!*

Next to us, a guy in shiny basketball shorts is doing the same to Jeremy.

"Noooooooo!" Jeremy cries, just like Darth Vader in *Revenge of the Sith*.

I know he's trying to make me laugh, but I don't have

the energy. Outside the arena, the master computer has tallied those final shots and decided that Clip's team is the winner. For the *fifth* time in a row. I press my hands over my eyes. Maybe if I lie here long enough, I'll melt into the mats and they'll forget about me.

The music stops and the lights turn on, signaling the end of the game. All around us, kids climb out from their hiding places, wearing the regulation helmet, vest, and shin and elbow guards. They crawl under nets and over railings, talking and laughing as they make their way through the maze of blue mats to the exit.

Iggy Morales jogs over to us, his dark brown skin gleaming with sweat. He's a big, bulky kid and one of Clip's soccer buddies. "Hey, Sadie, Jeremy, I'm sorry I left you guys in the lurch back there," he says. He points to a mess of ropes and nets in one corner of the arena and quirks an eyebrow at Clip. "*Someone* shoved me into that, knowing I'd get stuck."

"Well, I had to take out the strongest player on your team, didn't I?" My brother crosses his arms over his chest and smirks down at me. "Tough luck, sis. Time to do the walk of shame."

I reach out and grab my own knee. Sometimes it's got a mind of its own, and my brother and his tenders are right within kicking range.

"Good going, man." Shiny Shorts takes off his helmet,

showing off his messy, sandy-blond mop of hair and twinkling blue eyes, which make my cheeks feel warm. Derek Marshall is twelve and going into the seventh grade in the fall, just like Clip. He lives next door, plays basketball with no shirt on in the summer, and has been best friends with my brother for as long as I've been alive. I'm okay with all of the above . . . except maybe the best-friends-with-my-brother part.

"Aw, I didn't do much," Clip says modestly.

"You came up with an awesome plan." Derek's twin sister, Caroline, removes her helmet, too. Today she's wearing skinny jeans and her nails are painted neon blue. "Making noise like we were being attacked, while really we were lying in wait the whole time? Brilliant."

Seeing how cool she looks makes me want to disappear into the mats again. I wanted to impress her and Derek so bad, but now they probably think I'm just a silly kid for losing.

Clip puffs out his chest. "Little Sadie here still has a lot to learn about strategy."

"If you can call puppy-guarding the goal a *strategy*," I snap, but he and Caroline are busy bumping fists with the other sixth graders, and he doesn't even look at me.

"Sadie's strategy was good," Jeremy speaks up, loyal to the end. "She was going to sacrifice herself so I could climb up the tower. That takes guts."

"It does take guts. And hey, laser tag is just a game. You'll get us next time." Derek grins at me and holds out his hand to help me up. "You and Darth Vader here nearly made it."

My insides feel like ice cream left in a hot car. "Thanks," I say, trying to stay casual. He doesn't need to know I am never, *ever* washing this hand again. I can still feel his fingers when he pulls away to help Jeremy to his feet.

"We're not going to be defeated for long," Jeremy vows. "This is just like the Battle of Helm's Deep, when Aragorn, Legolas, and Gimli all thought they were done for."

"Helm's Deep is that fortress King Théoden owned, right?" Derek has seen the Lord of the Rings trilogy with Clip and me a zillion times and knows exactly how the story goes. But he still listens as Jeremy blabbers on excitedly about dark lords and wizards all the way to the exit.

Outside, the control room looks fake bright after the darkness of the arena. A bored high school dude with potato chip crumbs on his lip collects our equipment. Beside him is the master computer that monitors the entire game and tracks points. Our vests send information to it whenever we've been hit by an enemy laser.

"Looks like Team Scissors wins again!" my brother

gloats, looking back to make sure Jeremy, Iggy, and I have seen the score. The 150,000 points under his team's name—inspired by his nickname, Clip—show that they not only got *their* President to safety, but they also vanquished every one of their enemies. Us.

Iggy just shakes his head and walks out the door, unbothered by my brother's bigheadedness. But Jeremy sees my clenched fists and puts a hand on my shoulder. "We might have only scored ninety-five thousand points, but I wouldn't count Team Foehammer out just yet."

"Yeah. Keep telling yourself that, kid." Clip swaggers out into the lobby with Derek and Caroline, not bothering to hold the door for us.

"You know, your brother's kind of a jerk when he's around his friends," Jeremy says.

"You're only noticing that now?" I say grumpily. Clip at least says "Good try" or something else nice if I lose to him playing video games at home. A couple of years ago, when we got along just fine, he might have even wanted to be teammates with me. But these days, when he's around his cool friends and has a reputation to keep up? No way.

It's a rainy Saturday, so the Lase-Zone lobby is packed with kids, and all of them seem to know my brother. He high-fives some guys on his soccer team, waves at a blushing red-haired girl, and chats up a couple of eighth graders before he even walks ten steps. He's been even more disgustingly popular ever since Coach Katz named him this year's soccer MVP for Saybrook Middle School. And I know it will only get worse if he gets the captainship next fall, which would make him the first-ever seventh-grade captain at the school.

I roll my eyes and glance out at the parking lot. A conveyor belt of cars is dropping kids off and picking them up, like clockwork. My phone buzzes in my pocket, and I pull it out to see that Grandpa's text is literally all emojis. There's a car, a skull and bones, a dancing lady in a red dress, a puppy face, and a monkey covering its eyes.

"What does that mean?" Jeremy asks, peering over my shoulder.

"I've created a monster," I mutter. Emojis have been a sort of secret language between Grandpa and me ever since my parents gave me my first phone last year. I remember it being a lot more fun to try to decode each other's messages then, but now I wish he would just type out what he wants to say. "I think the car one means he's here."

I glance outside again, and sure enough, Grandpa's dark blue Honda is inching forward in the vehicle parade outside. I turn and yell for Clip, but he's busy talking to the enormous circle of friends around him about some online game they play.

"*War of Gods and Men* later?"

"Oh yeah! The dragon world is awesome so far!"

"I leveled up last night—I'm a pig-riding mage now. It's pretty sweet."

"I know! Dude, when I saw you attack that city . . ."

Jeremy drifts toward them, his eyes wide. "I'm hoping to be a mage soon, too," he says, but they all ignore him.

"Hey, *Clarence*, are you listening?" I say loudly. "Grandpa's here."

Clip scowls, as he always does when I use his real name in public. "I gotta go, but I'll talk to you guys tonight," he tells his friends.

I tug at Jeremy. "Come on, we'll give you a ride home."

CHAPTER TWO
SADIE

CLIP PULLS OPEN THE DOOR OF GRANDPA'S CAR AND
flings himself onto the passenger seat without saying
"Shotgun," like you're supposed to.

"Shotgun," he says out the rolled-down window, seeing my mouth open to protest.

I throw him a dirty look, then climb into the back seat,
where our golden retriever is waiting. "Hi, Tofu," I say,
kissing his nose. He pants and slobbers all over me, then
puts a massive paw on my shoulder to tell me he's happy
to see me. Clearly, he's my *nice* brother. Then he clam-
bers over me to lick Jeremy's face, too. "Grandpa," I
say, as the car pulls out of the lot, "you gotta text me
words, okay? It's like reading hieroglyphics whenever
you message me."

"But it makes sense," Grandpa protests. "You got the

car and the dog, right? The lady is Grandma, and the skull is us if we don't get back in time for dinner." He laughs at his own wit, then peers at us in the rearview mirror. "You guys have fun today? Did you win?"

Clip snickers, but I ignore him as I buckle my seat belt. "We lost, but yeah, it was fun."

"It was great, Grandpa Tran," Jeremy says brightly. My grandparents always tell him to call them Grandma and Grandpa like Clip and I do, or Bà ngoại and Ông ngoại, the Vietnamese versions. Jeremy likes to add their last name at the end to distinguish between them and his own grandparents. "Sadie carried me on her back at the end like a champ."

"She's strong like an ant," Grandpa says fondly, and Jeremy and I do a jellyfish, which is our special version of a fist bump where we wiggle our fingers as we pull away. Clip snickers again as our car merges into traffic, and Grandpa side-eyes him. "Winning is not important anyway. Just a game. Grades are more important. Right, Clarence? Where is your report card?"

"Yeah, *Clarence*," I chime in, delighted. School is the one thing Clip can't beat me in.

"There's still a week left before summer vacation." Clip would *never* whine like that in front of his friends. "We don't get report cards until the last day of school."

"I hope it is all As, like Sadie's will be." Grandpa's eyes crinkle at me in the mirror. He and Clip look a lot alike, except Grandpa smiles at me way more. "And Jeremy, too."

"All except gym, but yeah." Jeremy scratches Tofu behind the ears, oblivious to the fact that his black *Firefly* T-shirt is completely covered in yellow dog hair. "Hey, Sadie, want to come over and work on that social studies assignment tomorrow? Ruth said we could order a pizza."

I nod at once. Jeremy's parents are doctors and are always away at conferences and stuff, so we get their whole house to ourselves. And Ruth, the housekeeper, doesn't care what we do as long as we don't mess up their library. "Can you give me a ride there, Grandpa?" I ask.

"Sure. I'll give you money for the pizza, too." He waves away Jeremy's protests. "I insist. One day, you can pay me back when you're a doctor like your parents."

I groan, but Jeremy just smiles politely. My grandparents are cool and even make fun of themselves sometimes for being old-school, but the whole doctor thing? Where they try to get Clip, me, and all of our friends to go to medical school? I get the feeling that's not really a joke. "You need to stop watching *Grey's Anatomy*, Grandpa," I tell him.

"That is a very good show!" he protests.

We drive past a huge construction zone. The Lucky Lion Supermarket, an Asian grocery store Mom and Grandma used to shop at, is now gone. A couple of months ago, when Mom and I drove by to buy my graduation shoes at DSW, the site had looked like a pile of rubble. But today a new, gleaming building is there, with shiny glass windows and a freshly painted roof.

I press my nose against the window, staring at the giant sign attached to the fence that surrounds the property. "Blackwood Gaming Arena," I read aloud.

"Restaurant, bowling, mini-golf, an arcade, and . . ." Clip whirls around to look at Jeremy and me, forgetting to be cool.

". . . Laser tag!" we all say at the same time.

"Grandpa, slow down!" I beg.

"I cannot. There is a very angry Massachusetts driver behind me," Grandpa says, peering nervously at the rearview mirror. He starts ranting about aggressive Boston drivers, but none of us are listening to him.

I poke Jeremy. "I bet that arena's bigger than a football field!"

"It looks *so* much nicer than Lase-Zone."

"Are you kidding? The school *cafeteria* is nicer than Lase-Zone. We just didn't have anywhere else to go . . .

until now." Clip cranes his neck, trying to get another look, but we're already too far away to see the building. "Let's go *there* for your graduation dinner, Sadie."

I start to agree, but then stop myself. Clip's a pickier eater than I am, so Grandma and Grandpa *always* let him choose the restaurant when they take us out to eat, even on my birthday. I do want to check out the new place, but I have to put my foot down. It's *my* graduation dinner, after all. What's that word Ms. Clayton taught us in social studies? *Principle*, with an *-le* at the end. "It's the principle of the thing," she had said.

"Nah, I still want to go to Zucchini Garden for my dinner," I tell him.

"But I don't *like* anything at Zucchini Garden! It's all gross pasta and stuff . . ."

I wish I could record him on my phone whining for all his popular soccer friends. "Too bad. I'm the one graduating, not you. It's the principle of the thing," I add, for good measure.

"Grandpaaaaaaaa!"

Grandpa makes an annoyed *tsk-tsk-tsk* noise with his tongue. "You two, stop fighting in front of your friend. You will be in the same school soon. Is this how it will be?"

"No," I say, at the same time Clip says, "Yes." We glare at each other.

I'm mostly excited to start sixth grade at Saybrook Middle in September. But I'm not looking forward to sharing the halls with my brother. He'll probably pretend we're not related.

That's a game two *can play*, I decide, scowling.

Tofu senses my mood, like he always does. He climbs off Jeremy and heaves his giant bulk into my lap to cuddle, nearly dying in the process because Grandpa suddenly hits the brakes, *hard*. I throw my arms around my dog, one hand clenched on his Star Wars collar.

"What in the tarnation is she doing?" Grandpa shouts. He must have learned that from one of those old cowboy movies he loves. I would laugh, except we just nearly killed a person.

We've turned down a side street, and a woman has run right in front of our car. Even though *she* wasn't paying attention, she glowers at Grandpa and raises her hand in the air.

Quick as a flash, Clip reaches back to cover my eyes.

"What are you doing?" I screech, slapping away his sweaty palm.

"She's making a bad hand gesture! Don't look!" my brother says.

"Clip, we've *seen* that before in movies," Jeremy says gently, like he's talking to an agitated toddler. "We'll be fine. And anyway, she's just giving us the what-the-heck hands."

The woman scowls at us through the windshield with both palms turned up to the sky. She's white, with blond hair so light, it looks gray. Her lime-green jumpsuit is several sizes too small and clashes horribly with her aqua sneakers. She mouths something at us.

"She's blaming *you*, Grandpa! Even though she was the one who ran in front of the car!" Clip says angrily. He leans over and gives the horn a good long blast.

"Clip! Stop that!" Grandpa scolds him. "It was just a mistake."

The woman looks like she might come around to Clip's window and yell at him. But then she rolls her eyes and slouches away.

"Nobody yells at my family for no reason and gets away with it," my brother says darkly.

Grandpa reaches over to tousle Clip's hair. "Forget it. No reason to be upset," he says, then shakes his head and keeps driving. "She's going to get herself killed one day."

"She was coming from the direction of that new gaming arena," Jeremy says. "Maybe she got distracted, thinking about how awesome it's gonna be." And as easy as pie, he's made us all cheerful again. We forget the woman and start discussing laser tag.

Soon, we pull in front of the Thomases' beautiful three-story brick house. "You sure you don't want to have dinner at our house, Jeremy?" Grandpa coaxes. "Grandma Tran made pho."

Jeremy practically drools at the mention of my grandmother's specialty dish. It's a hot Vietnamese soup of thick noodles and rich beef broth, and you get to add all kinds of yummy things: black pepper, green onions, bean sprouts, lime juice, or spicy chili sauce. "Pho, my favorite," he moans, pronouncing it the way we've taught him: like *fuh*, with a question mark at the end. "But I promised Ruth I'd come home for meat loaf. Sorry, Grandpa Tran."

"Don't be sorry. Come next time, okay?"

"I promise I will! See you tomorrow, Sadie!" Jeremy gives Tofu another pat and climbs out of the car, waving to us before he slips through the front door.

"I worry about him. Home alone all the time with only the housekeeper," Grandpa murmurs as we drive off. "Mom and Dad always gone."

"It's a busy life, being a doctor," I say slyly, catching Clip's eye. It's one of the few things we can agree on these days: my grandparents being ridiculous for wanting *us* to be doctors. I can't look at a paper cut without feeling woozy, and Clip is too lazy to tie his shoes, let alone perform a heart transplant. "I don't know if I'd want to be away from my kids so much."

Grandpa waves that off. "You could take them on nice vacations," he says breezily, and Clip rolls his eyes at me. "Or you could buy a laser tag arena."

"So she could lose even more than she already does?" Clip cackles. And just like that, we've gone from being on the same side to being opponents again.

I lean against Tofu, remembering how amazing the Blackwood Gaming Arena looked. It's going to be a clean slate for me, I decide. New day, new rules, new arena.

Soon, I'm gonna prove to Clip I can be just as good at laser tag as he is.

CHAPTER THREE
CLIP

ON MONDAY, EVERYONE ON THE BUS IS TALKING about the new laser tag arena. The fourth and fifth graders who go to Steeplebush Elementary School are listening to some kid brag about his contractor dad working on the building.

"He told me it's *three* levels high, and it's got a whole tunnel maze and a twisty slide. It's state of the art," he's telling them all proudly, as I make my way to the back.

The bus stops at the elementary school first, so the little kids sit in front and the sixth, seventh, and eighth graders get the seats way in back. My stomach clenches when I see Derek, Caroline, and Iggy sitting with an eighth grader named Ben Anderson, who has snagged one of the best seats: the short one right over the back bus wheel.

A few years ago, some kids broke into Mr. Green-Myers's laptop and posted photos of his grading spread-sheet on social media. People made fun of me for *months* because I had the lowest math score in the entire third grade, and Ben was one of the ones who bullied me the hardest. That whole mess is why I threw myself into soccer, so I could be the best at *something* and no one could tease me about it. Since then, Ben and I have acted like it never happened, and I pretend to like him because he's captain of the soccer team.

But I haven't forgotten.

I relax when I see that Derek's saved me the other seat. I always feel a little lighter when my friends show me that they like me. Kids are high-fiving me and saying, "Congrats on the game!" and inviting me to their pool parties all the way back, and I remind myself: *You're cool now, Clip. Forget what happened in third grade.*

"Yo! This ain't a runway, hoss!" Fred, the bus driver, yells down the aisle at me. "Quit your sashaying and sit down."

Everyone laughs, but it's nice laughter, like they're saying, "That's Clip for ya!"

I do a little shimmy for ol' Fred's benefit and take my spot, bumping knuckles with everyone around me. The bus wheels squeal as we pull away from the curb.

"What's going on, team? How was the rest of everyone's weekend?" I ask.

"I was just telling *them* I rode my bike over to that new Blackwood arena yesterday." Ben flicks his head toward the twins and Iggy. He has this way of lifting his chin, so he's looking at you down the line of his nose. Like you're a piece of fuzz on his sock that could be either a dust bunny or an evil blood-sucking spider.

"And?"

"*And*," he says, rolling his eyes, "it's everything that little pip-squeak up front is saying. I couldn't get close 'cause of the chain-link fence, but I saw awesome stuff through the windows. Tilted floors and a rock-climbing wall and weird mirrors, like in a funhouse."

"It sounds amazing," Caroline adds, her fingernails digging into the cheap brown plastic of her seat. "We are never playing at Lase-Zone ever again."

"That place *sucks*," Iggy agrees, even though he'd had just as much fun as any of us on Saturday. "This one's gotta be a zillion times bigger and better. Do we know when it's opening?"

"I don't know about you guys, but *I* know." Ben's smile reminds me of the purple cat in that weird old Disney movie Sadie likes. The one where the girl falls down a hole and talks to a caterpillar, and there's a bunny rabbit running around with a clock. What's it called again?

"When is it opening?" the twins demand.

"I think a better question would be *why*." Ben's gaze sweeps around to each of us, and I can tell he's enjoying this. "My mom's got some dirt on the woman who owns the place, and she'll be reporting it on the eight o'clock news tonight. Make sure you tune in."

We wait, but Ben only hums an Imagine Dragons song, tapping his fingers to the beat.

"So . . . the woman?" Iggy prompts him.

"What? Oh yeah!" The purple-cat smile crosses Ben's face again. "Apparently she was some tech big shot out in Silicon Valley. She worked for a huge company and made a lot of game apps and also created this special virtual-reality version of laser tag. But she quit when her son died under mysterious circumstances. I guess she came out here to start over."

I cross my arms. "Mysterious circumstances, huh? Like what?"

"Nobody knows," Ben says, looking at me like I'm hopelessly stupid. "That's why they're *mysterious*, duh."

"Who cares?" Caroline asks. "The important thing is, when does this place open?"

"Friday. *This* Friday." Ben wiggles his eyebrows. "Who's up for skipping class that day?"

And for one absolutely wild moment, I consider it. My science quiz is on Thursday, which means Friday will be a day for goofing off. All I'll have is art, gym, study hall, and social studies with Mr. Alles, which everyone knows is a total joke. But I can't risk Mom and Dad finding out, not with summer vacation starting soon.

"Friday *night*," I say.

"What's the matter?" Ben drawls. "You chicken? Even a fourth grader knows it's gonna be jam-packed that night." He leans forward, and we lean with him automatically. "We have to go during the daytime. That's when it'll be empty and all ours to explore."

The Marshall twins look at each other. Derek's not a bad student, but Caroline's a flea's breath away from flunking science and I'm right there with her. If we get in trouble, it's on our record, and I can't let anything get between me and the captainship of the soccer team. I want to take Ben's place in the fall, and Coach Katz is almost as serious about grades as my parents are.

"*You* got nothing to lose," I say, studying Ben. "This is your last week of eighth grade, and then you'll graduate and go to high school. But us, we got two more years. I don't know about anyone else, but if I get in trouble, there goes soccer for me."

As soon as I say it, I get this wiggly feeling in my stomach. Almost like the pho noodles I ate yesterday are still there and alive. But this kid's getting on my nerves, and I *hate* when people try to push me around. So I make sure not to blink or look away as Ben stares me down.

"I agree with Clip," Derek says, and I feel this wave of relief. He's probably worried about their dad shipping Caroline off to summer school as punishment, but still. "Maybe you can go during the day on Friday and let us know what you think."

"You sure Chu here's the only Asian?" Ben sneers. "Seems to me you all care about school way too much." Everyone gasps and turns to stare at me, to see what I'll do next.

My face burns. I get a flashback from third grade of Ben hovering over me, sneering that he didn't know Asians could fail math class. There's a feeling like a can of soda in my chest has been shaken, but before it has a chance to explode, my sister appears. I hadn't even realized she'd been listening. She stands in the aisle, one skinny arm braced on her hip and the other against a seat to keep her balance. The bus driver hollers at her to sit down, but she ignores him.

"You shut your stupid, racist mouth," Sadie tells Ben fiercely. Somehow, she manages to look and sound just like Mom. "I oughta wash it out with Purell."

My jaw drops, and across the aisle, Ben's wearing the same expression.

"I can help you out there, Sadie." Caroline, looking furious, whips out a tiny bottle of clear stuff from her backpack and waves it in Ben's face.

"News flash, not everyone who cares about school is Asian," Iggy says angrily.

"And there's nothing wrong with caring about school anyway," Derek adds.

Ben smirks, but his face and neck have gone bright red. My friends have my back, and he can't do anything about it. "Whatever, little Asian nerds." He stands up and shoves past Sadie so hard, she nearly falls into Derek's lap.

"What the H-E-double-hockey-sticks is going on back there?" the driver yells at us.

"Anderson," I say, and something in my voice makes Ben stop and turn back. His small blue eyes are mean but curious. This is a side of myself I have always been careful not to let him or anyone on the team see. "Apologize to my sister."

He looks like he's about to make a snappy retort, but then he looks down at Sadie. My sister is sitting next to Derek, looking even smaller next to him with her face tomato red, and I think about how much it must have taken for her to stand up for me. I get up and take a step toward Ben. I'm twelve and he's almost fourteen, but we're the same height, five-six.

The bus is a sea of open-mouthed faces, all watching us. I can hear some of the fifth graders quietly chanting, "Fight, fight, fight."

Ben sizes me up, then glances at Sadie again and mutters, "Sorry," as though he's suddenly realized he knocked over a little girl. Then he moves up a couple of rows and plunks down beside one of his eighth-grade buddies. They start whispering, and I know I haven't seen the end of this yet. I sit back down in my own seat.

"That's more like it!" shouts Fred the bus driver, nodding at us in the rearview mirror.

"Are you okay?" I ask my sister gruffly.

"Are you hurt?" Caroline asks at the same time.

"I'm fine," Sadie says, then gives a little sigh and starts to go back to her seat.

"Just stay there," I tell her. "We don't want Fred to freak out again."

"Really?" she squeaks, looking at me from the corner of her eye. "It's okay if I sit here?"

Her shock makes me feel like the meanest brother in the world. "It's okay," I say, and when she smiles, I add, "But only for today, and only because I need to ask you a question."

Sadie raises her eyebrows. "What?"

"You know that whacked-out cartoon you like? The one with the singing flowers and the caterpillar that smokes a pipe?" I ask, remembering Ben's purple-cat grin. "What's it called?"

"Oh my *god*," she groans, as the others laugh. "How many times do I have to tell you? It's *Alice in Wonderland*."

This time, we all smile.

CHAPTER FOUR
CLIP

"I CAN'T EAT ANOTHER BITE," JEREMY GROANS, rubbing his bulging belly, though he's still eyeing the plate of Vietnamese summer rolls. They're like egg rolls without the crunch: shrimp, noodles, and fresh mint rolled up in sticky rice paper, dipped into a sweet and spicy peanut sauce. "That was so good, Mrs. Chu."

Mom beams. "I'm glad you liked it. I'm not much of a cook, but anytime one of my mother's recipes works out, I call that a win." Her eyes cut to me, even though my phone is on my lap where she can't possibly see it. "No texting at the table. Put the phone where I can see it."

"Dinner's almost over," I argue, but plop my phone on the table anyway. My parents may be millennials *and* first-generation Vietnamese Americans, which means they're easygoing for the most part, but that doesn't mean they can't be as tough as Grandpa and Grandma sometimes.

Everyone watches my phone light up five times. Two texts from Iggy; one from Brad, who wants to make laser tag plans; one from Pete; and one from Amy, this girl I'm kind-of-sort-of going out with. My fingers twitch, longing to read the messages, but Mom's still watching me like a hawk, so I sigh and turn the phone over.

"So, what are your wild Thursday night plans, kids?" Dad asks cheerfully. "I hope you won't be bored without the grandparents around to spoil you."

Grandpa and Grandma have a bingo tournament tonight, which I hate (because normally they would take us out for ice cream) but Sadie loves (because if ultra-traditional Grandma were here, she would make her help clean the kitchen, being a girl).

Mom and Dad both look at me, and so do Sadie and Jeremy, and I feel a wave of annoyance. Why do I always have to entertain little kids? I just want to be alone. I want to go into my room, shut the door, and blast music while I fight dark forces on *War of Gods and Men* with all my friends. My mind races through a list of possible excuses.

"I have to study" won't work, because my quiz was this morning.

"I need to do homework" also won't fly, because Mom and Dad know me too well.

And somehow I don't think "I have a war to wage against the orcs" will pass, either.

"Why don't you watch a movie?" Mom suggests, as she and Dad get up to clear the table. "Or I can give Clip some money to take you out for ice cream."

"It's okay if Clip's too busy," Jeremy says quickly, seeing the look on my face. "Sadie and I were going to go ride our bikes anyway."

I yawn and reach for my phone, and even though Mom is at the sink with her back to me, she says, "Don't even think about it, Clip. Go with them." The woman has Spidey senses.

Sadie sweeps some crumbs off the table for Tofu, who hustles forward and vacuums them all up. "We'll be fine, Mom. We were just going to check out that new laser tag place."

That gets my attention. "But it's not open yet."

My sister shrugs. "We'll just look in the windows. Evan—that kid whose dad worked on the building—said there's an actual train you can ride in there. We wanna see if he was lying."

I forget the texts piling up in my phone for a second. "Maybe I *will* come with you."

"Yeah, do it!" Jeremy says. "We might see them getting ready to open tomorrow."

Within minutes, we are all wearing helmets and biking back to the Blackwood Gaming Arena. It's about a fifteen-minute ride, and when we get there, the place looks the way it did when we drove past on Saturday, except shinier. The doors and windows gleam in the setting sun.

We drop our bikes on the grass and peer through the chain-link fence. For a big-time family center that's about to open, there sure isn't a lot of activity. We don't see anyone in the windows. Not a single soul is sweeping, polishing, or carrying stuff. It's kind of eerie, actually.

"Our school could probably fit in there three times," Sadie says, awed.

"There's the slide Evan talked about," Jeremy says, pointing to a structure made of bright red plastic. It spirals from the top level all the way down to the ground level. To the left of it, an entire wall is covered with weird rippling glass. "And those are the funhouse mirrors."

"There's no train, though," I say. "Maybe it's farther in, with the laser tag arena."

"Do you kids like what you see?" someone asks.

We all spin around to see a very tall lady in a bright

purple long-sleeved dress that comes down to her ankles. She's wearing a silver necklace with a charm that looks like a gingerbread house. She looks older than Mom and Dad but younger than Grandma and Grandpa, and she's pretty, with thick gray hair in a bun, bright green eyes, and smooth, papery skin.

"Yes, ma'am," Jeremy says politely. "We're excited for it to open tomorrow."

The lady tilts her head, looking at the building like she's trying to imagine seeing it the way we do. "Do you want to come inside and have a look?"

Sadie looks up at me like Mickey Mouse just offered her an apartment at Disney World. "Oh, can we?"

"Is that allowed?" I frown, looking up at the lady. She's almost a head taller than me.

"If I say it is." She winks, holding out a long hand with fingernails painted glittery dark blue. "I'm Mardella Blackwood, founder and creator of the Blackwood Gaming Arena."

My mouth falls open. From what Ben told us, I pictured someone short and wiry with thick-rimmed glasses, kind of like Mrs. LaFevers, my science teacher. This lady looks like she stepped out of one of those fancy magazines with the weird clothes that cost a fortune.

We remember our manners and shake her hand. Sadie

introduces all of us, eagerly adding, "Would you mind showing us around, Ms. Blackwood?"

"It would be my pleasure. And please call me Mardella." The lady pulls out a key and unlocks a swinging gate in the fence, leading us across the parking lot to the main doors. "Feel free to give me your honest opinions. I want this place to be the most fun I can make it."

We follow her into the lobby and gasp at the sight of it. The walls are painted bright blue and covered with cool game and movie posters. There are comfy suede couches everywhere and wide-screen TVs hooked up to a dozen different gaming consoles. Pinball machines and old-fashioned arcade games like *Pac-Man* and *Tapper* line the walls. The gleaming front desk doubles as a phone-charging station, and there's a snack bar that will serve pizza and milkshakes.

"What's that for?" Jeremy asks, pointing to a device that looks like a heavy-duty printer, except it has three scanner guns at the front. It's connected to a wide-screen monitor on the wall.

"Ah! That's for these." Mardella reaches behind the desk and holds up a stack of small, white plastic cards. "Every player will get one of these, with a barcode that's unique to them. Every time they play a game, whether it's mini-golf or bowling or laser tag, they'll scan in and the card will track every point they earn. They can win fun prizes and see their name up on the digital leaderboard." She gestures to the wide-screen monitor. "That will display the top ten winners in any game and can be accessed online, so people can check the rankings."

I'm practically sweating. This woman just literally said all of my favorite words. "So what kind of fun prizes do the winners get?"

"Well, I don't want to spoil too much for you," she says, her eyes twinkling, "but one of the prizes is a whole week of free pizza and milkshakes. Or you might even get a month of free games, depending on how far up the leaderboard you are."

Jeremy and Sadie look at each other excitedly.

"Those are just a couple of examples. My chief operating officer, Naima Dennis, will be in charge of running the arena from day to day, and you're going to love what she's cooked up."

"*You're* not going to run the arena?" Sadie asks.

"I'll be here only to consult and help out. I designed everything, so now I get to sit back and watch you kids have fun. At least, I hope you will," the lady adds, smiling as she toys with the charm on her necklace. Up close, I can see tiny colorful jewels that make up the candy roof and candy windows of the gingerbread house. It's whimsical and creative, just like her arena.

I rub my hands together, cackling. "Are you kidding? Of course we'll have fun. Wait 'til Ben finds out I saw all of this before he did!"

Mardella smiles. "Is Ben a friend?"

"Not really," I admit, feeling mad again when I remember what he said on the bus. But I forget him when Mardella points out the bowling alley, which is about the size of a gym and has eight lanes. Next door is the arcade, where every game and Skee-Ball machine spits out tickets you can exchange for awesome prizes like sunglasses, stuffed animals, and small electronics.

"Just something to get you started." Mardella hands us each twenty tickets, and I'm liking her more and more. She shows us the restaurant, which is circular with a glass ceiling so the sun can come in. The mini-golf area loops around it, so people eating can watch the action.

Sadie clasps her hands together. "Could we please see the laser tag arena?"

Mardella laughs. It's a nice, cheerful sound. "I'm glad I saved the best for last! The control room is over here." She snaps on a light, and it feels like we are standing inside a blockbuster sci-fi movie. The walls, floor, and ceiling are made of shiny steel. The biggest computer

I've ever seen takes up one entire wall, surrounded by smaller computers.

"Why are there so many machines?" Jeremy asks.

"Good question. I've created a unique arena that allows several games to take place at once. Each of the small computers monitors one game, and the master computer tracks all of them." Mardella leads us into a wide hallway filled with cubbies. "Players wear protective gear and a vest with strike zones, just like in other games. The helmet is where it becomes different." She hands each of us a helmet, with three adjustable buckles instead of one.

"Wow, they're so light!" Sadie says. "Featherlight."

Mardella helps us put them on and shows us how the opaque black visor swivels down over our eyes. "These are virtual-reality headsets. Laser tag in my arena is not just about firing phasers at your enemies. It's also about the experience. With these helmets, you will instantly be transported . . . almost to a different world." She looks down for a moment, and her smile is sad.

"What do you mean, 'transported'?" Sadie asks.

Mardella clears her throat. "Well," she says, press-ing some buttons on a remote control, "you can choose from a variety of laser tag games. You can play classic laser tag, *or* you and your team can undertake a series of quests in one of six battlegrounds."

"Whoa!" I cry out. My visor has suddenly flashed on, like a little TV screen, and I'm standing in a dense green forest. I see Mardella, Sadie, and Jeremy just like normal, but the cubbies and the computers have turned into trees and shrubs. There's grass under my feet and a cloudy sky overhead. I can practically hear birds calling to each other in the treetops.

"This is *seriously* cool," Sadie says in a hushed voice.

"Normal objects around you will become part of your surroundings," Mardella explains, as Jeremy bends down to touch a (fake) shrub. "You can explore the Enchanted Forest, which is where you are right now. Or you can search for gold in the mountains." Buttons click, and in a flash the forest disappears and we are on a rocky cliff, hundreds of feet above the ground.

"It's like Lord of the Rings," Jeremy whispers. One-track mind, that guy.

Mardella clicks a few more times, and the scenery switches through a few different backgrounds. "I've also designed other simulations, including a haunted castle, a mad scientist's basement lab, and a jungle swamp. You can remove your helmets now."

"This is unbelievable," Sadie tells her. "You are going to make *so* much money."

The woman laughs. "Making money isn't as important

as knowing my guests are having fun." She replaces our helmets in the cubbies. "I can't let you into the arena itself today, since we're in the final stages of beta testing. But if you come over here, you can take a look inside."

We follow her to a long window overlooking all three levels of the laser tag arena. The ground level is a labyrinth of thick rope nets and blue padded walls, perfect for hiding and spying on enemy teams. It looks like an obstacle course, with a rock-climbing wall, dangling ropes, and even a little platform you can stand on and pull yourself to the upper levels using heavy cords.

Jeremy and Sadie pepper Mardella with eager questions, but I press my nose against the window, dying to dive right in. I can already see myself flying down the twisty slide, crawling through the tunnel maze, and swimming in the ball pit. Soon, "Clip Chu" is going to be the name at the top of every leaderboard in this arena.

"Why are you smiling like that?" Sadie demands, coming over to me.

"Because I'm happy and excited for my free week of pizza and milkshakes, duh."

My sister crosses her arms over her chest. "You're *that* sure you're going to win it?"

"Have you seen me play?" I ask incredulously. "Of

course I'm going to win it. Don't worry, sis, I'll share the wealth with you."

"And what if *I'm* the one who wins it?"

I turn to look at her scrawny self and almost burst out laughing, but I decide not to. The look on Sadie's face is one I would describe as *dangerous*. "Well, we'll just have to wait and see, won't we?" I say instead, trying to sound as wise and big brotherly as possible. But something in my voice seems to annoy her as much as if I *had* laughed, and her eyes narrow to slits.

"You don't think I can do it," she hisses. "You don't think I'm good enough."

"Hush, I'm trying to listen to Mardella. She's telling Jeremy something interesting," I say, to put a cork in the argument before it starts up again.

Truth is, I'm the best laser tag player in the Chu family, no contest. But my little sister isn't bad. Sometimes she's a little bit too *not bad* for my taste. My stomach clenches again, like it did on the bus when I was remembering third grade. Except this time, I'm thinking of my birthday party last year. It was at Lase-Zone, and Mom insisted that I let Sadie and Jeremy join in. I won every game, of course, but a few of them were close calls. *Too* close.

Sadie's department is school, and mine is sports and

athletic stuff. So why does she keep trying to barge in on *my* territory? It's not like I invade hers.

Annoyed, I turn my full attention to Mardella, who is explaining the ins and outs of the arena to Jeremy. "Certain parts of the floor will shift and tilt, to make it feel like you're walking across a rocky surface," she's saying. "And we've set up air-conditioning units and fans to act as wind, and there are heat lamps if you pick the swamp and cliffs quests. I've also designed areas with plenty of olfactory and auditory simulation, too."

"Olfa-what?" I ask.

"Smells and sounds. You might smell grass or rain or musty books, and you might hear birds or bubbling potions or a waterfall, depending on what game arena you pick." She chuckles. "We've thought of everything here. Well, what's the verdict so far?"

We all start talking excitedly, and Mardella holds up her hands, grinning.

"This makes me very happy. To thank you for coming along on my tour, here's a little something for you and your friends. Tell everyone about it." She gives us each a bunch of 50 percent off coupons for entrance. "I hope to see you all tomorrow or this weekend."

"Oh, we'll be here tomorrow night," I promise.

"As soon as school is out," Sadie adds, pocketing her coupons. "We'll bring everyone."

"Well, *good*! It was a pleasure meeting all of you. Do you know the way out?"

Jeremy nods. "Thanks again!"

Sadie is back to her normal cheer as she and Jeremy chatter excitedly all the way out the exit.

I follow them, but just as I am stepping back into the lobby, I glance over my shoulder into the control room. Mardella is still standing by the window where we left her. She is looking down into the arena with that same sad smile, her eyes searching the levels like she's lost something there that she can't find again.

CHAPTER FIVE
SADIE

"SO, WHAT'S THE BIG DEAL WITH LASER TAG ANY- way?" Dad asks, as he's driving Clip, me, and all of our friends to the Blackwood Gaming Arena on Friday night. "You guys seem very excited about it, but isn't it a little . . . old-fashioned?"

"Old-fashioned?!" we all repeat, shocked.

"No way, Mr. Chu," Jeremy says. "This place is going to be high-tech and advanced."

"It's virtual reality," I add. "We told you, Dad, remember? There are visors you wear to feel like you're right in the battleground itself."

"It's action-packed and fun," Derek chimes in.

Dad turns right at the traffic light, and we see a long line of cars ahead of us, waiting to get into the arena. "I believe you. But laser tag was something we did for fun back in *my* day."

Clip, who's sitting in the passenger seat, gives him a look. "Your day was, like, ancient Rome. Laser tag's changed a lot since then."

"Oh, come on, it wasn't *that* long ago! I bet your old man can still impress you. How about it? I'll find a parking spot and come in and show you guys my funky moves?"

"Dad, *please* no!" my brother and I both say in alarm.

"Why not?" Dad asks cheerfully, looking at everyone in the rearview mirror. He puts the car in park as we wait and starts moving his arms around like he's a broken robot. It takes us a second to realize he's pretending to do kung fu. "I'd kick some serious butt, right, Jeremy?!"

"Sure thing, Mr. Chu," Jeremy agrees weakly from the back seat.

"Dad, pleeeeeeeease," I beg, covering my eyes as Iggy and the Marshalls laugh.

"I'm about *this* close to just getting out of the car right here," Clip declares.

"Pew, pew!" Dad says, doing a little shimmy of his shoulders while pretending to fire a laser. "See? I could still play. Pew, pew!"

"Dad, stop! You're not coming with us!" Clip almost screams, pulling the hood of his sweatshirt over his eyes.

"What's wrong, son?" Dad teases, poking him in the ribs. "Am I embarrassing you?"

"Father, please move the vehicle forward," I say in as calm a voice as I can, as our friends cackle at his ridiculousness. I don't mind that Dad is a total goofball . . . *most* of the time.

"Indeed I shall, daughter," he answers in the same formal voice, and finally we inch closer to the entrance. "I was just messing with you. Have fun and be safe! I'll be back at nine."

Everyone piles out of the car in front of the gaming arena, Clip and me leading the way with relief and our friends chorusing, "Thanks, Mr. Chu!"

We enter the arena, and the lobby is *packed.* There are people everywhere, sitting on the comfy couches, ordering milkshakes at the counter, and wandering in and out of the arcade. A bunch of kids yell excitedly as they wave handfuls of tickets in the air, while a big group of older teens heads toward the mini-golf arena with clubs and colorful golf balls in hand.

"I wonder if we'll see Mardella again," Jeremy says.

"I think we'll have a hard time finding her, even if we look," I reply.

"That's so cool that you guys got to meet the owner," Derek says, as we join the long line at the front desk. "Did she give you any tips and tricks?"

It was a joke, but of course Clip takes it seriously.

"Even if she tried to give us pointers, I'd tell her no," he scoffs. "When I win, I want it to be on my own steam." His eyes are on the wide-screen monitor that shows the digital leaderboard. There are already four or five winners' names listed in each category, and as we watch, #3 Lorien L. (who has 1,303 points) switches positions with #2 Jessica R. (who has 1,287 points) on the list for mini-golf.

"There's no one listed for laser tag yet," I say, standing on my tiptoes so I can see.

My brother smirks. "Keep your eye on that number one spot."

"I *will*," I tell him, annoyed by his tone. "Can't wait to see my name there."

"Oh, *please*, Sadie. You would need a miracle."

"It could happen, you bighead! I've come close to beating you before."

Clip spreads his hands. "When? Where? I need some proof so I—"

Iggy rolls his eyes and moves to stand in between us. "Oh, break it up, you two. Let's just have fun tonight instead of launching the Chu-pocalypse again."

"Seriously," Caroline agrees, slinging an arm around Derek's neck. "You two need to take a leaf out of me and Derek's book. You don't care if I beat you at laser tag, do you, D?"

Her twin shrugs. "Not if you share the prize, *especially* if it's pizza."

Clip and I scowl at each other, but we let it go . . . for now. Not even Caroline gets what it's like to be me. *Her* brother is nice, and their relationship's different 'cause they were born five minutes apart. Clip is a year and a half older than me, and lately, he acts like he learned all the secrets of the universe in that time. He thinks I'm slow and weak and uncoordinated, but I'm going to show him I'm every bit as good as he is.

"Hey, look, there's a list of prizes next to the leaderboard," Jeremy says, trying to distract us, and it works. Because when we scan through the dozens of awesome rewards—including 10,000 arcade tickets, a $50 restaurant gift certificate, and your own special mini-golf club engraved with your name—we see what the ultimate grand prize is.

"Oh my god! How come Mardella didn't tell us this place was part of JCD Universal?" Clip almost shrieks, his eyes bugging out at the sight of the familiar TV network logo. Right below it is a familiar-looking poster of two muscle-bound warriors surrounded by witches, warlocks, elves, and other magical characters. Iggy and Jeremy and Derek are all flipping out, too, and dancing in line. "The grand prize winner gets a part in the *show*?!"

"Okay, that's pretty cool," Caroline says, looking impressed.

"Wait, I don't watch a lot of TV. What show is this?" I ask, confused.

"*War of Gods and Men*!" Clip, Derek, and Iggy all shout at once.

"JCD Universal is a whole media empire, Sadie!" Jeremy explains, quivering with excitement. "They're right up there with ABC, NBC, and those guys. They make a ton of video games, too, and I guess there's gonna be an adaptation of *War of Gods and Men*!"

By this time, we've reached the front of the line, and the lady behind the counter is grinning as she listens to our conversation. She's short and pretty, with deep brown skin and close-cropped curly hair. Her name tag reads "Naima Dennis, Chief Operating Officer."

"It's actually not an adaptation, but a reality TV competition inspired by the game!" she tells us. "Think *American Ninja Warrior* or *The Amazing Race*, but with high-fantasy obstacle courses."

"What? That's amazing," Derek says, as Clip's jaw drops.

"Kids can compete, too?" Iggy asks quickly.

"There's going to be three versions: a show for grown-up contestants, one for teenagers, and a junior version for kids between the ages of ten and thirteen. Which I guess applies to all of you," Ms. Dennis says, laughing as everyone cheers. She hands each of us a white plastic card with a barcode on it. "Go ahead and scan these into the computers, type your name, and get your picture taken. Then you'll be in the system and ready to hit that leaderboard!"

"You can say that again!" Clip says enthusiastically.

"Luellen over there will help you if you have any trouble," Ms. Dennis says, and Clip, Iggy, and Caroline rush to follow her instructions while Derek, Jeremy, and I hang back.

I study the poster while we wait. I'm the only one in our group who doesn't play *War of Gods and Men*, but competing in a high-fantasy obstacle course on TV sounds very cool—and would *definitely* be the kind of thing that would earn my brother's respect. I imagine galloping on a horse and firing a bow and arrow as a studio audience screams, *Sadie Chu! Sadie Chu!*

"What do you have to do to win the grand prize?" Derek asks.

Ms. Dennis is busy helping the next people in line, so Jeremy answers. "Looks like you have to be the top scorer at the Blackwood Gaming Arena by June 30," he says, squinting at the fine print. "That's only weeks away!

I'm guessing you can play anything that will earn you points . . . laser tag, mini-golf, Skee-Ball. But you have to be number one out of *everyone*."

"That's how they get people to come back," I say. "Pretty clever."

Jeremy, Derek, and I march up to the scanners next. There's a staff member standing nearby, a thin white woman in her forties with grayish-blond hair. She looks *so* familiar, but I can't remember where I've seen her before . . . until my eyes fall on her aqua-blue sneakers. And then I realize she's the weird lady who ran in front of Grandpa's car the other day! Clip is too busy staring around the lobby, but Jeremy recognizes her, too, and elbows me in the side.

We hold our barcodes under the laser. The machine gives an electronic *beep!*

"Nice job, kids," the lady says, looking a lot friendlier. There's a name tag that reads "Luellen B., Staff," pinned to her navy polo shirt. "Go ahead and type your names into the keyboard, first and last. And then stand over there for your photos. Are you excited for tonight?"

"Yeah. The arena looks great," Jeremy says politely.

"What will you play first?" Luellen gives us such a welcoming smile that I start warming up to her a bit more. Maybe she was just having a bad day that other time we saw her.

"Laser tag, definitely," I say.

We type in our names and stand on red Xs on the floor. The camera snaps our photos.

"That's a great choice. I recommend the Space Station simulation. I hear the line isn't as bad as, say, the Haunted Castle or the Swamp." Luellen lowers her voice. "Plus, there's a *huge* bonus in the Space Station if you keep your eyes peeled. But you didn't hear that from me."

Derek, Jeremy, and I look at each other eagerly. "Wow, thanks!"

"Move it, guys," Clip calls to us, already pushing his way through the crowd. "The line for laser tag is ridiculous and I want to play at least two games before we leave."

"A huge bonus?" Jeremy asks, as we hurry after my brother. "What could it be?"

"No idea. But I want it," I tell him.

He grins. "How about we team up and get on that TV show together? Think we can?"

"Oh, I *know* we can!" We do a jellyfish fist bump, and I'm feeling more excited by the minute. Because there's only one thing better than rubbing victory in my brother's face . . . and that's rubbing victory in my brother's face with my best friend.

O━◀

I am standing on an alien planet, about to go down the three-story twisty slide.

"I bet the last moon-rock is down there," I tell Jeremy, who is examining some of the dangling ropes. Unlike the helmet at Lase-Zone, this helmet holds his curly cloud of hair nicely. It has room for my ponytail, too, and feels both light and comfortable.

"I already searched the entire ground level," Clip says behind me. "I didn't find anything. I think we should check the area by the funhouse mirrors again." He swings his phaser from left to right, as though a moon-rock might appear at any second.

We've taken Luellen's advice and used our 50 percent off coupons on a team quest in the Space Station battleground: locating five magical moon-rocks hidden somewhere in the arena. In order to win, according to the staff member who prepped us, we have to: 1) find all five blue moon-rocks first (the other team's are red) and claim them by firing a laser at a target painted on them, and 2) take out every member of the other team by striking each of their vests three times.

"You guys come with me," Clip says in his bossy voice. "I need your eyeballs."

I sigh. Earlier, when we were waiting in line to play, Iggy borrowed some straws from the restaurant so we could draw them to pick teams. Unfortunately for Jeremy and me, Clip ended up with us. My brother's been nicer ever since I told off that nasty eighth grader on the bus, but here in the game arena? With victory at stake? He's back to being his old self.

"I think it makes more sense if we split up," I argue. "Jeremy can stay up here, I'll sweep the ground level again, and you go look at those mirrors."

Clip opens his mouth to complain, but a flash of movement appears in the corner by the emergency exit. "Get low," he warns us, angling his phaser in that direction.

The music isn't as loud here as it was at Lase-Zone, but I can still feel the heavy bass pounding in the padded pillar that Jeremy and I duck behind.

A figure appears and fires a laser at Clip, who flings himself onto the mats just in time. "Run! Save yourselves!" he roars at Jeremy and me. "I'll find you later!"

We obey immediately. We've each been hit by an enemy laser twice, but my brother's only been struck once. One by one, we lower ourselves into the twisty slide. It's a fun, dark, slippery ride, and I have to keep from laughing or shouting out as I twirl around the twenty seconds it takes to get to the ground floor. No need to give off our position to the enemy.

On the bottom level, Jeremy catches my eye and jerks his head toward the elevator platform. I nod and he jumps on it, pulling himself silently to the second level.

"Okay," I whisper. "If I were a moon-rock, where would I hide?"

My visor shows a rocky and treacherous terrain, full of crevices and craters and lit by an eerie futuristic glow. Surrounding me is the cold, empty blackness of outer space, but once in a while, a shooting star will pass by or a bloodred planet will swivel through on its orbit. Mardella's simulation is so realistic, it's almost scary. The pounding music adds to the spooky environment, because it keeps me from hearing any enemies sneaking up.

Laser tag is all about staying alert, all the time.

I swing my phaser from side to side, enjoying how light it feels in my hands compared to the bulky ones at Lase-Zone. A headpiece buzzes inside my helmet.

"I made it to the second level," Jeremy's voice says in my ear.

I grin. That's another perk the Blackwood Gaming Arena provides: walkie-talkie communication via the helmets. "Ten-four, Mithrandir," I say, using his code name. It's one of the aliases of Gandalf the Grey, the wizard from Lord of the Rings . . . of course. "Do you see anything up there?"

"No. Be careful. There's at least one enemy with Clip, but the others might be with you."

"Roger that." I stand in a corner, phaser up and back protected, scanning my surroundings. There's no sign of life whatsoever. "I'll let you know if I see anything."

"Good luck, Samwise. Mithrandir out."

A second later, my headpiece buzzes again, and this time, it's Clip. "I'm by the funhouse mirrors. I'm okay," he says smugly. "That was Iggy. I hit him right in the chest."

"Nice," I say, my eyes roving up and down the wall next to me. Maybe a moon-rock is attached to it somewhere.

"Derek and Caroline might be near you, so watch out. We got one moon-rock left."

"I know, I know. Quit yammering—I need to focus."

Thankfully, Clip shuts up, and I duck and run, making sure to skirt the wall. This helps me keep my bearings and also protects me on one side. Clip might be the athletic one in the family, but I'm pretty fast, too. I make it to the other side of the arena in under a minute.

I stand in front of what looks like low shelves of rock,

jutting out at weird angles. I lift up my visor for a second, to see what I'm *really* looking at, and it's a tangle of mats and nets that form the entrance to a small crawl space. I shift the visor back down over my eyes and drop to the floor on my stomach, inching forward with my phaser pointing in front of me.

"Here goes nothing," I mutter, crawling into the low tunnel.

Something flickers in my field of vision. I freeze, eyeing it. As I watch, it moves slightly to the left and disappears. I crawl forward, following a twisting, low passage shaped by the nets. Hopefully it's not a dead end, because I could be cornered by whoever's down here with me.

On the other hand, the fifth moon-rock could be here.

It's this thought that keeps me squirming forward slowly, imagining myself leading our team to victory. I *have* to show Clip that I can be just as good as he is.

The flickering thing appears again, this time on my right. I freeze, staring at it. This time, it doesn't go away. It just stays there, casting a pale light on the mats around it.

Could it be the fifth moon-rock?

My headpiece buzzes, and Jeremy's voice quivers with excitement. "Sadie! I found the fifth moon-rock!"

Guess not.

"Also, Clip just took out Iggy and Derek in one fell swoop," he continues. "There's only Caroline left, so get your hobbit butt up here."

"I can't talk," I whisper, as quietly as possible. My phaser slips in my sweaty hands. "I think she might be down here with me."

"Oh, man. Be careful. Meet me on the second level when you can. I'll wait."

The whole time, the flickering object hasn't moved. It's about thirty feet away, nested in a corner formed by two joined mats.

I know it's not the moon-rock, and now I doubt that it's Caroline, either. She wouldn't stay in one position in a dead end; she'd be a sitting duck. If I were smart, I would ignore whatever this is and go meet my team-mates on the second level so we can win this game. Not to mention the darkness and the cramped, closed-off space are making me a little uncomfortable. Can I even find my way back out?

But something tells me to go check out the flickering, so I do. Maybe Mardella has programmed an extra challenge into the simulation. If this is the "huge bonus" that staff member Luellen was hinting about, I could earn a ton of points right off the bat and get a head start on Clip. Inch by inch, barely breathing, I crawl toward it . . . and then I stop dead.

It is a boy.

He glows eerily in the darkness, and he is not Iggy, or Derek, or Clip, or Jeremy. He is *no one* I know. And his whole body is shimmering. He's lying flat on his stomach with his face pressed to the mat. Is he sick? Has he passed out?

"Hey," I call, but there's no reaction.

He shouldn't even be in this section of the game arena. The Blackwood Gaming Arena rules are that each group stays in their own reserved sector, so they can't interrupt or get distracted by other players and other games happening at the same time. Somewhere above us, I hear kids yelling, laughing, and having fun—other teams and other quests going on.

Maybe this boy got lost and ended up in our section somehow.

"Hey, are you okay?" I say, a little more loudly.

Slowly, he lifts his head and looks right at me. His face is glowing and as white as a ghost's. But the creepiest part are his eyes: wide and black, with no white parts.

"Help me," he whispers. "Please."

And then the outline of his body goes fuzzy, and he vanishes.

CHAPTER SIX
CLIP

"DUDE, YOU ALREADY GOT ME." IGGY'S VOICE IS muffled because I've tackled him onto his stomach and his face is pressed into the floor. By my hand. "Just let me up."

"I have vanquished you, alien enemy! Now I'm gonna take your whole planet!" I let go of him and climb to my feet, grinning as he turns over and rolls his eyes.

"Man, you are *intolerable* when there's a game at stake."

I whistle. "Look who's pulling out the SAT words, and we're not even in high school yet. Catch you on the flip side, bro." I hum the theme to *The Avengers* under my breath as I hook my phaser onto my vest and wrap my body around a fireman's pole. In the simulation, it's supposed to look like a creepy space beanstalk or something.

I slide down to the second floor of the arena and shift my phaser into defensive position again.

I feel like an action hero in a sci-fi movie, defending my team against the hostiles who want to take our spaceship. Kind of nerdy, I know. That's usually Sadie and Jeremy's territory. But it helps me whenever there's a game I need to win. That's why I'm so awesome at soccer.

I stop humming, because Caroline could be anywhere. She's been struck twice—once by Sadie and once by me, and Jeremy's found the fifth moon-rock. All we need is to find and hit Caroline with a laser one more time to win the whole thing.

Three strikes, you're out.

The second level of the arena is designed to look like an abandoned space station. Sort of like from that old movie *Alien* Grandpa likes so much. The floors, walls, and ceiling are all steel-plated with rivets, and the lights are flickering overhead, casting shadows everywhere. Every now and then, steam erupts from a vent in the wall. I feel a blast of hot air and remember Mardella telling us how she's put in smells and sounds to help the quest feel even more real.

I can't help lifting my visor a few times to reassure myself I'm in a laser tag arena.

Wherever Caroline is, she's well hidden.

I crouch under a bank of spaceship controls and push a button on my helmet. "Jeremy. Where are you?"

"Code name is Mithrandir," he reminds me cheerfully. "And I'm in the space suit vault."

That was the area where we found the first moon-rock, behind the twisty slide in a thick curtain of space-ship cables and wires (just pieces of glittery felt dangling from the ceiling. I lifted my visor to make sure). The vault is a round room with a bench in the middle and giant sheets of glass displaying old-fashioned space suits.

"What are you doing?" I ask impatiently. "We're supposed to be looking for Caroline."

"I know, but I heard someone calling for help. I think there's another kid here."

"You sure it's not Derek messing around?"

"No way. It didn't sound like him." There's a long pause. "Oh . . . oh no."

"What is it?" I ask, but there's no response. "Jeremy? Mithrandir? Come in."

There's only silence, and my heart picks up. He and Sadie might be goofing around, trying to make me nervous, but he sounded almost . . . scared. I force myself to grin and crawl out of my hiding space. Teach me to play laser tag with a couple of babies.

And speaking of Sadie, where is she anyhow? Jeremy's told us both that he found the moon-rock in one of the Space Station's drawers. She should be up here, helping us find Caroline.

I crab-walk with my back to the wall, head swiveling from left to right. Part of why I'm so amazing at laser tag is that I've studied my opponents.

I know Sadie is small and fast and likes to hide close to the ground. Iggy and Jeremy are on the bulkier side, so they depend on the element of surprise rather than speed. Derek always tries to climb and find higher ground, where he can see the lay of the land better.

But Caroline's a tricky one. She's small and fast like Sadie, climbs even better than her twin, and also enjoys the element of surprise. She could jump out at me from a corner at any time. She might even be watching me somewhere, getting ready to pounce.

I find an alcove designed to look like an astronaut's sleeping area and climb in. "Sadie?" I whisper. "Sadie, come in. Where the heck are you?"

"Still on the ground level." My sister's voice sounds odd, too. Scared, like Jeremy. Maybe this arena is too much for them. "I . . . I found a kid. He was asking for help."

I raise my eyebrows. "Another one? Jeremy said he heard someone asking for help."

Sadie gasps. "Was it that same boy? He looks like he's part of the simulation. I think he's been programmed into the quest or something."

"He wasn't real?"

"No, he got all fuzzy and disappeared. He's . . . he's probably just part of the game." She doesn't sound convinced. "Okay, I'm crawling out of this creepy place. I'll get on the elevator and find my way up to you."

"All right, be careful."

A light above me flickers, then goes out completely, sending this part of the spaceship into almost total darkness. Something is shimmering in the far corner of the room. I squint at it, but it's definitely not Caroline. We're all experienced laser tag players, so we always wear dark clothing. Whatever—or whoever—that is looks to be wearing a light-colored shirt. Really dumb, considering all the black lights in the area ready to light you up.

I think for a second. The area where the shimmering thing is looks wide-open. It would be risky to check it out, with nobody covering me from behind. Caroline could be lying in wait.

Then again, it sounds like Mardella *did* put some Easter eggs or something in the simulation. I wouldn't put it past her; she's pretty much proved to all of us that she's a genius at designing laser tag quests, and Sadie and Jeremy mentioned that a staff member hinted about a huge bonus. Whatever it is, it's got my name written all over it.

I try to buzz Jeremy again, to see if he can cover me. "Mithrandir, come in. Do you hear me?" But there's still no answer and I start feeling worried for real. Did something happen to him? If Caroline took him out, he would at least let me and Sadie know.

I growl with frustration. I can't just sit here when there's a game to be won. And I *really* want to check out that glowing thing, because if it really is the bonus, it *has* to be mine.

Slowly, I step out of the alcove, arms over my chest to protect my strike zone. I wait a full thirty seconds, but there's still no movement and I relax a bit. Caroline could be hanging out on the ground level. As I stand looking at the glowing thing, I notice an odd object attached to the ceiling. It's too dark to be sure, but it almost looks like a video camera pointing right at me.

"Security, maybe," I mutter to myself.

Still, the thought of someone watching me is a little uncomfortable—as is the fact that both Sadie and Jeremy mentioned a kid asking for help. No one else should be in this sector except for my friends and me. But if he *is* part of the game like Sadie thinks, that would confirm that Mardella has added bonus features to each quest.

Feeling a bit bolder, I start striding over to the shimmering object.

"Ha!" Caroline yells from behind me, and I jump a foot and nearly drop my phaser. But I recover quickly and pivot on my back foot, aiming right for her chest. We both strike each other, right on the target, and our aim lands true.

A robotic female voice announces through the speakers: "Blue Team wins. Please shift your visors to standby position and make your way safely to the exit."

"Yeeeeahhh!" I scream, pumping my fists in the air. I pull up my visor and grin at Caroline, who is shaking her head. "How does it feel to be the losing team for once? Huh?"

"I got you, too," she says matter-of-factly. "And I had just found my fifth red moon-rock on this level right before I ambushed you."

I give her a golf clap, lightly tapping the fingers of both hands together soundlessly.

"Why'd you come out of hiding anyway?" she asks.

That's when I remember the shimmering thing. "I saw someone . . . some*thing* in that area over there." But of course, now that the lights are on and our visors are up, it looks like a regular laser tag arena again and the corner is empty. "Jeremy and Sadie were saying something about a kid who shouldn't have been in our section. He kept asking for help."

Caroline's blue eyes widen. "So that *was* someone crying by the tunnel maze! I thought I was hearing things, because it stopped when I asked if they were okay."

We head back out to the twisty slide, and I tilt my head up at the ceiling again. Just as I thought: a black video camera is swiveling on the ceiling, following our movements. There's a blinking red light on one side.

"Maybe they're recording videos for YouTube or something," Caroline says with a shrug when I point it out to her. "It could be for promotion. Or for safety, in case anyone gets hurt and they need to send staff to them quick."

"It still creeps me out a little," I admit. One by one, we go down the slide and meet up with everyone else on the ground floor. Jeremy is the first person I see. "Hey, what happened to you? I couldn't communicate with you anymore."

"Sorry," he says sheepishly. "Somehow the microphone got dislodged in my helmet and I had to hide somewhere to put it back together."

Derek heads over to us from the fireman's pole, followed by Iggy. "What was all that about some kid crying, Caro?" he demands.

"You saw him, too?" Sadie and Jeremy say together,

staring at Caroline. They each share their story of seeing the strange boy.

"It was probably just part of the game, like you all said," Iggy tells them, removing his helmet. "There might be extra tasks that pop up when you're done with the main ones. Maybe you were supposed to find him again and see what he needed."

Sadie shudders, and it bothers me a little bit. My sister's a pretty brave kid and doesn't get shaken easily. "His eyes were so freaky. I'm probably going to have nightmares about it tonight. You guys didn't see or hear him at all?"

Iggy, Derek, and I shake our heads as we remove our gear, piling the helmets and phasers alongside one wall like we're supposed to when we're done playing.

"Come on," I say, slinging an arm around Sadie's shoulders. "Maybe some strawberry milkshakes will help you forget him. But hey, this is the best laser tag arena *ever*, right?"

Everyone except Sadie starts talking enthusiastically about their favorite moments. She glances back over her shoulder like she might see that weird kid again.

CHAPTER SEVEN
SADIE

"GOOD MORNING, GRADUATE!" DAD SINGS WHEN I
come into the kitchen. The whole house smells like butter and cinnamon, and there's a giant, cheesy balloon that says *ConGRADulations* tied to my chair. Grandma beams as she arranges a bouquet of hot-pink daisies, my favorite, in a vase and Grandpa captures my reaction with his phone.

Mom turns from the griddle and smiles approvingly. "You look so grown-up, Sadie!"

For fifth-grade graduation, I am wearing a sleeveless white dress that comes to my knees. It's covered in sky-blue flowers that match my headband, and I'm carrying strappy black shoes with a tiny heel that I will put on later (since we never wear shoes inside, to keep the house clean). I twirl in place for everyone, and my grandparents applaud.

Clip is already eating at the kitchen table. He's got a plate of white rice sprinkled with soy sauce and topped with three runny fried eggs. "Do you want a Vietnamese breakfast or an American breakfast?" he asks me, bright yellow yolk dribbling down his chin.

"Why?" I ask, sitting next to Dad and pushing away the balloon so it doesn't make my hair staticky. "Are you gonna cook it for me? Also, close your mouth when you're eating."

He charmingly opens it wider so I can get a good look at all the half-chomped eggs and rice in it. Why every girl in the sixth grade is in love with my brother, I'll never know.

"You should see your brother fry an egg," Grandma says proudly. She brings over a plate of the waffles Mom's cooking and puts them in front of me, then pats Clip's shoulder. "He's so smart and good at everything he does."

I bite down my reply that frying an egg isn't rocket science when Mom catches my eye and gives me an understanding smile. When *she* was growing up, Grandma raised her to fry eggs, make her own bed, do laundry, and vacuum, while Mom's older brother did nothing but play video games and get praised whenever he bothered to fold one towel. Mom always told me how hard it was at times growing up in a traditional household, and she gets how unfair it is that Grandma thinks boys and girls ought to be treated differently.

But at least Grandma is trying hard to change, because she sees the look between Mom and me and quickly adds, "Sadie's smart and good at everything *she* does, too."

"She is," Mom agrees, bringing me a jug of Vermont maple syrup and kissing the top of my head. "Graduating elementary school with a perfect record. We are so proud of you, kiddo."

"You will be a *sixth* grader after today," Grandpa tells me happily, waving the chopsticks he's using to eat his syrup-drenched waffles. He and Grandma eat *everything* with chopsticks, including spaghetti and mashed potatoes. "You are grown up now, Sadie. You should start thinking about what you want your career to be."

Dad raises an eyebrow. "It's a little early for that, Pop, don't you think?"

"It's never too early to think about your future. She should find out what she wants to study. Maybe you'll go to Harvard Medical School, huh, Sadie?"

"She's only about to start middle school. There's plenty of time to figure out what she likes and wants to do," Dad tells him, with the slightest edge to his voice. "I don't believe in pushing kids to make these big decisions before they even hit high school."

I don't say anything as I eat my waffles, but I lean against Dad and feel him relax a little. When he was a kid, his parents pushed him *hard* to become a doctor and threatened to cut him off if he studied anything else. They didn't end up doing that, even though Dad's an accountant now, but their relationship has never been great . . . which is why Dad is super protective of Clip and me, and our right to do whatever we want.

"At least she can think about what colleges she likes," Grandma suggests.

"*If* she even wants to go," Dad says firmly. "College isn't for everyone, and there are people who do very well for themselves without higher education."

Grandpa and Grandma just stare at him, and Mom quickly steps in like she always does when she senses tension between them. "Can we all stop talking about Sadie's future, please?" she jokes. "I only get to keep both of my babies for six or seven more years, and I don't want us to get too far ahead of ourselves."

"All right, fine. But Sadie can be whatever she wants to be," Grandma says.

Dad and I exchange glances. "Wow. Thanks, Grandma," I say, stunned.

"She can be a doctor, a lawyer, or an engineer," my grandmother continues, ticking off the items on her fingers. "Whatever she wants, we will support her."

"There it is," I mutter, and Mom puts a hand on Dad's shoulder to keep him from getting annoyed again. She heard this speech constantly while growing up, but her parents weren't as intense as Dad's, and now she works as a website designer.

Dad clears his throat, changing the subject. "I made the reservation for Zucchini Garden tonight at six, Sadie. Maybe after dinner you can pick a movie for all of us to watch together."

"I hope it will be a Western movie," Grandpa tells me eagerly.

"A Western movie?" I repeat. "You mean, an American movie?"

Clip swallows a mouthful of food. "Western as in chaps and tumbleweed," he clarifies. "Not Western as in the opposite of Grandpa."

I take a sip of my orange juice. "Maybe, Dad. We were thinking of playing laser tag again with our friends, weren't we, Clip?"

Mom carries a plate of thinly sliced fried Spam to the table and lays a few pieces on Clip's rice. "You guys have been playing laser tag quite a bit, haven't you? That can't be cheap. Maybe it would be nice to take a break tonight."

Clip gives her his most winning smile. "But, Mom, think about how proud you'll be when I score a zillion points and get on TV! And anyway, we got more fifty percent off coupons for winning our game last night. We're actually saving a ton of money."

Grandma nods her approval. "I like that. Maybe Grandpa and I should come, too."

I look at my brother, alarmed by the image of our grandparents trailing after me in the arena, complaining about the darkness and the loud music and yelling that I'll break my neck if I keep running like that. But as usual, Clip's got this handled.

"It might not be a good idea, with Grandpa's high blood pressure," he says smoothly. "And the arena's really loud and stuffy and full of kids."

"Fine, fine," Grandpa says mildly. "I'll drive you after dinner."

When breakfast is over, Clip and I wait on the lawn while Dad backs the van out of the garage. Derek, who's helping his dad mow their lawn next door, jogs over. I wave, trying to act casual, but my hand goes a little out of control and whacks the fence, and my cheeks burn.

"You okay, Sadie?" Derek asks.

"Stop being strange," Clip tells me, bumping fists with Derek. "You up for laser tag tonight, dude? I texted some guys on the team and they're all coming."

"I'm in! But Caroline can't." Derek sighs. "Mrs. Rivera called Dad. Apparently Caro failed her last science test and she's grounded for a week."

"Dang, seriously? That sucks."

"Whatever, it's her own fault. I guess that means Sadie will be representing the girls tonight," Derek adds, smiling at me. "I hope you're coming with us?"

Thought #1: I'll be the only *girl*?!

Thought #2: Derek wants me to come?!

"Uh, yeah. Yeah," I say, as my entire vocabulary disappears from my head. So much for all those As in English. "I'll come with you."

"Awesome. Maybe we can do the Haunted Castle simulation this time." His dad yells for him to come help. "I gotta go, guys. Congrats on graduating, Sadie. See you both tonight!"

I try to nod and wave, but in front of Derek, my brain can only do one thing at a time. So I end up doing this weird wink/shoulder lift.

Thankfully, Clip doesn't notice my awkwardness as we climb into the van. "The Haunted Castle was the one I wanted to do next, too. There's eleven of us, including you and Jeremy. If we're on different teams, I'll let you have the extra player. You guys will need it, and . . ."

I tune out his blabber all the way to the elementary school. Half of my brain is still by the fence with Derek, and the other half is imagining what the Haunted Castle simulation will be like. Probably even creepier than the space battleground.

That gets me thinking about that strange boy again. What kind of weird thing was *that* to program into a game? It had nothing to do with laser tag or with space. Why would Mardella bother putting him in . . . unless it was somehow important?

"You know that jerk on the bus? The racist eighth grader?"

Clip finally stops running his mouth. "Ben? What about him?"

"He said his mom is a news reporter and she's got dirt on Mardella Blackwood. Like, how she left California after her kid died." I chew on my bottom lip. "What did the kid look like?"

My brother looks at me like I'm nuts. "Why does that matter?"

"Remember that boy Jeremy and I saw? And Caroline heard him crying? I'm wondering if Mardella programmed him in as sort of a weird . . . like, tribute to her kid or something."

"You think she coded an image of her dead kid into laser tag?" Clip's voice isn't as mocking as I thought it would be. He actually seems to be considering it. "I wonder what we were supposed to do. Maybe if we figured it out, it might unlock a bonus level or something."

"Maybe. I bet that's what Luellen, that staff member, was trying to hint about."

Clip tugs at the tie Dad made him wear. "I hope we see him again tonight. We'll find out what it's all about, and maybe we can even ask Mardella about it, if we see her."

"Ask her about her kid? No way." I shake my head. "If it's a test, we'll have to figure it out on our own."

Dad parks the van and we all walk into the brightly lit elementary school gymnasium. The place is packed with families and graduating fifth graders carrying balloons and bouquets. A couple of volunteer parents hand Mom, Dad, and my grandparents each a flyer with the program and the students' names printed on it. Some teachers usher the families to the metal bleachers, while others round up the graduates in the hallway outside by alphabetical order.

Jeremy and I do our jellyfish fist bump as he's passing by on his way to the back of the line. "Laser tag tonight?" I ask.

He gives me a thumbs-up. "Ruth can give me a ride."

Honestly, I'm still creeped out about the weird boy. But at the same time, I'm excited to play. I stink at team sports, so laser tag is as close as I get to what Clip must feel whenever he's on a soccer field. Like I'm on an important mission . . . like I could surprise myself anytime.

Principal Hopkins clicks past in her high heels, beaming, and the third- and fourth-grade orchestra strikes up an off-key version of "Pomp and Circumstance." One by one, we march into the gym and a hundred phones and cameras snap photos all at once. Grandpa, unsurprisingly, is not sitting with Mom, Dad, Grandma, and Clip like he's supposed to be. Instead, he's fighting off three teachers so he can stand right in front of the bleachers. "Just one picture. She's my only granddaughter," he tells them, aiming his phone at me and clicking it at least a dozen times. "Sadie! *Sadie!* It's Grandpa. Look over here! Look here!"

"That's your grandpa?" whispers Erica Davis behind me.

I pull my hair in front of my burning face and nod.

"Don't sweat it. My stepdad's in the back waving a poster board he made of my face, so I feel you." The procession takes us to a dozen rows of folding chairs, and she sits next to me.

"I'm glad we're going to middle school. I bet they don't do cheesy graduations like this."

We chat as our class takes their seats, and I don't feel so lonely anymore without Jeremy. Erica's always been nice, but she mostly hangs out with the art and theater kids.

An idea occurs to me. "Hey, are you into laser tag? A bunch of us are going after dinner. You could come if you want, since we have an odd number for teams right now."

Erica's light brown eyes widen. "Hey, that sounds cool!"

I know she means it, but I also know Clip is a big reason she's saying yes. She keeps darting glances at him in the bleachers. As I watch him, he lets out a huge yawn and starts picking his nose. Like I said . . . I don't know why everyone has a crush on him. Oh, well.

"We'll meet there at seven thirty."

Erica nods, her strawberry-blond pigtails bouncing. "I'll be there!"

"AND A DAY MAY COME WHEN OUR COURAGE FAILS!"
Jeremy roars, pacing across the swinging bridge with his
fists clenched. "A day on which we are faced with dark
forces! When a shadowed road lies before our hungry
eyes!"

"This kid should never, *ever* be captain of anything,"
my friend Pete whispers.

"Agreed," Brad and I say in low, toneless voices.

"Remind me who died and made him King of the
Geeks again?"

I cross my arms. "The stupid straws. The stupid straws
that don't deserve milkshakes."

Before entering the arena, we had drawn straws to
determine teams and choose team leaders. Somehow,
Sadie's nerdy best friend pulled the longest straw for our
team, giving him the power to strut in front of us and

deliver this Tolkien-pumps-up-the-dudes speech. And my sister's not even here to help shut it down. She ended up on the other team.

Jeremy puts his fist over his heart, jaw quivering with emotion. "Friends, we must make the choice between what is right and what is easy. Will we forsake all bonds of team-ship?!"

"Okay, *now* he's just mixing up a bunch of different movies," I complain.

"Is *team-ship* even a word?" Pete whispers.

At last, Jeremy pauses for breath, winded from screaming lines out of every epic fantasy movie ever made, and I take the opportunity to jump in front of him.

"All right, people!" I bellow, enjoying everyone's eyes

on me. "The name of the game is Capture the Flag, Haunted Castle version. Locate enemy base, steal their flag, and bring it safely back to home territory. Three laser strikes lands you in the enemy's jail, and you can only go free when one of us risks our lives to save you. So don't go to jail!"

Jeremy, still huffing and puffing, reminds me, "Don't forget about the personal quest."

"Oh yeah. The personal quest!" I look each and every person in the eye. Besides Jeremy and me, there are four other people on our team: Pete, Brad, Greg, and Sadie's new friend Erica, who can't seem to stop giggling. "Tonight, the arena announced new laser tag bonuses: six Brass Keys, hidden somewhere inside the battle-grounds. If you find a key, it gets you an automatic fifty thousand points and a week of free milkshakes!"

Everyone cheers, including Jeremy.

I glance at the opposite side of the room. Our opponents are also listening to their captain, a kid named Hunter who does tae kwon do with Derek. I catch a glimpse of Sadie's ponytail.

A buzzer sounds in our waiting area. The staff member, a high school girl with purple streaks in her light brown hair, unlocks the gate leading into our assigned gameplay area. "All right, folks, you know the drill!" she says. "No physical contact, no food and drink, and no cell phones or other electronic devices inside at any time. If you need to leave, come back here and I will let you out. Hit one of the red buzzers only in an emergency, because doing so will stop gameplay immediately for everyone. Understood?"

"Understood," we chorus, and she slides open the gate for us.

"Visors down and phasers up, people! Let's go!" I scream.

It's like the Running of the Bulls as we charge into the arena, some of us already firing lasers at the other team. Pete and I drew up our battle plans on a restaurant napkin earlier, and I'm happy to see that my whole team is following them. Even Erica, the giggling girl, is all businesslike and looks back at me with a wave before disappearing.

The lights dim. Slowly, the game world unfolds before my eyes, thanks to my visor. We are standing on the mossy stone drawbridge of a seriously spooky castle. Ragged flags wave in the cold breeze (they are *not* messing around with the A/C in this place), and ghostly lights flicker in some of the windows. There's a speaker somewhere that plays the sound of loud, rushing water, and I peer over the side of the bridge to see a huge moat beneath me. I resist the urge to lift my visor and see what it really is.

There are twin towers on opposite sides of the castle. One has a purple flag—that's my team's home base—and one has a green flag, the one we need to steal.

According to the plan, Erica will scope out the enemy team's defense while Jeremy protects home base. Pete and Brad will be the attack team, stationed on different levels, and take out anyone they see. Greg, the fastest kid on our soccer team, has been assigned to be flag thief.

"What are *you* going to do?" Jeremy had asked me earlier.

"A little bit of everything," I had lied.

What I'm *really* going to do is find a Brass Key. My teammates have the flag covered, and I know victory is almost a sure thing. But glory . . . that's gonna be mine and mine alone.

I run into the great hall, which is full of dancing shadows from the torches. It's a tricky visual effect, because you don't know which is the shadow of a flame and which is of your enemy. The music is also louder than ever, so you can't hear much underneath the booming hip-hop bass besides an occasional shout.

There are four exits from this room: the door I came

through, a door up ahead, stairs going up, and stairs going down. I'm willing to bet no one's gone to the lower levels yet, because everyone's attention is focused on grabbing the other team's flag. My best guess is there's a Brass Key tucked away somewhere on the bottom level of the castle. A key opens doors, right? And where are there the most doors to open? The castle dungeons, duh.

Sometimes I'm amazed by my own genius. And they say Sadie's the smart Chu.

"Hey!" a guy yells. A beam of red light darts in front of me, missing my vest by inches.

I return fire and hear the satisfying *ping!* that means I've struck him. I hurry to the stairs and see that they end halfway down, and there's a rope ladder descending into the darkness. Without hesitation, I attach my phaser to my vest and grab the rope, climbing down nimbly. Whoever that guy was—it looked like Derek or Hunter—he probably saw where I was going. It won't be long before someone comes after me to look for a Brass Key, too.

I reach the bottom within seconds. The floor is simulated to look like stone, but it feels soft under my feet—padded mats, for safety. A torch flickers from around a curved hallway, and I follow its light cautiously, my phaser aimed outward even though I'm pretty sure no one else is down here. I hear yelling from the upper levels and hope Pete and Brad are living up to their big talk as our attack team. If they can take out our opponents and trap them in our jail, that will clear Greg's way to stealing the green flag.

I nearly trip over a beat-up metal chest just sitting in the hallway. "This is a *hazard*," I mutter, bending down to examine it. It's small, about the length of my arm from my elbow to fingertips, and it has a bunch of magnetic letters stuck all over the front, like a game of Bananagrams or something. I tug on the lid, but it won't open. "What even *is* the point of this?"

I shuffle some of the tiles around. I spell *look, cook,* and *dab,* and then I get bored and stand up. Stupid random chest. Word games are my sister Sadie's department, anyway, and I have more important things on my mind. Like finding the Brass Key and skyrocketing my name to #1 on the leaderboard.

Clutching my phaser, I proceed through the narrow hallway and enter the dungeon room. It's smaller than I thought it would be. It's a circular chamber with a couple of torches, and there are four prison cells with wooden doors. Each door has a window at about eye level, but when I try to peer inside, the light doesn't reach far and all I see is darkness.

If someone was standing in the shadows, I wouldn't be able to see them at all.

Something swivels on the ceiling, and I look up to see the familiar outline of yet another camera, the red light indicating that it's recording me. I give it a little sarcastic wave and do a jig for the benefit of whoever's watching me.

"Glad someone's documenting my truly awesome victory!" I shout.

A light catches my eye from one of the cell doors, and I recognize it at once as that weird flickering glow I noticed when we were playing the outer space simulation. A grin splits my face. This time, whatever it is, I won't let it get away.

I seize the door handle, half expecting it to be locked, but it swings open easily. The torchlight creeps in a little farther, cutting through the shadows, and I see a boy. He's about my age, and tall and thin and white, with feathery light hair. There doesn't seem to be any color to him, only a pale ghostly gray, and his outline flickers like he's a hologram. He's sitting with his back against the wall, his face tilted up to the ceiling, and his eyes closed. But he isn't relaxed at all—his hands are opening and closing into fists, and his face is all tense and frowning.

"Hello. I'm Clip," I say, taking a careful step toward him. He goes still. "Who are you?"

I wait, but he doesn't speak or open his eyes. His silent, motionless body is freaking me out a little bit. I remind myself that he's not a ghost, he's just a block of code inserted into the laser tag program. *If you want to be a game designer one day, you'd better toughen up*, I tell myself. Still, I wonder what I'd see if I lifted my visor. For all the fuzzy edges and flickering, the boy's presence seems so real.

"Uh, okay . . . my sister, Sadie, saw you the other day. She said you asked for help." I move closer, but his outline wavers and I step back again. "Don't go. I'm here to help you."

"How can you?" The kid's voice is soft and light, like fingertips brushing my sleeve, but somehow I can hear him clearly under the heavy beat of the music.

"I can do anything you need me to do," I tell him confidently, crouching down so I'm at the same level. "I'm the *best* laser tag player I know. What do I need to do to earn the bonus?"

Slowly, he lowers his chin, opens his eyes, and looks at me.

And even though Sadie warned me, nothing can prepare me for what I see. It's like looking at a bug. Where the rest of him is gray, his eyes are huge and black and shiny, with no whites. Regular eyes creep me out enough already, but with no white parts . . .

It takes everything I've got not to yell and run out of the dungeon. Instead, I stare into those blank, wide black eyes. *It's part of the game,* I remind myself. *And you've beaten way worse-looking bad guys in* War of Gods and Men.

"The bonus?" he repeats.

"Yeah, you know. The Brass Key?" I suggest.

"Oh. That." The boy tilts his head, studying me. "My name's Tom."

"Good to meet you, Tom." My hand flies out automatically to shake his, but I pull it back just as quick. "So, what are you up to in here? What's your story?"

"A witch trapped me in here. I'm cursed and I need your help." He says it in an almost robotic voice, like he's rehearsed beforehand. And is that a hint of sarcasm I hear?

Still, I nod, satisfied. "Okay, man, whatever you need. How do I help you? Do you want me to get you out of this prison cell, because, uh . . ." I gesture to the open door. "It's literally been unlocked this whole time."

Tom smiles bitterly. "I'm not trapped in this cell. I'm trapped in this *game.*"

"Oh, okay, now we're breaking down the fourth wall," I murmur. I've come across games like that before. I used to love this role-playing one where all the characters I encountered were aware that they were inside a game and that I was the player.

"And you *can* help me." Tom grunts as he climbs to his feet, his outline rippling like water. I get up, too, and see that we're about the same height and build. "Clip, right? That's your name? You need to come with me through this door, Clip."

And just like that, a second doorway appears in the wall of the prison cell. It's bright white, and its outline is fuzzy like Tom's. I feel a cold wind blowing out from it, ruffling my T-shirt. Tom steps in front of it and holds out his hand to me.

"Nobody else knows about this door," he says. "If you come with me, I'll help you win."

My ears prick at the sound of my favorite word, but something feels off about this. "Wait a sec," I say suspiciously. "Tell me more about this witch who trapped you before I come along."

"What?" he asks, looking annoyed.

I roll my eyes. "I need some backstory, bro. I'm not gonna go with you through some random door unless I know what I'm getting into." I wait smugly. I've played and beaten a *lot* of games in my time, and I know that these kinds of tests tend to reward the people who challenge them. One time, I sassed a troll in this online multiplayer game and he led me to an entire cave full of dragon's gold. I literally bought a castle with it and beat all my friends. "Tell me your story and what I'm gonna get out of it if I help you break this witch's curse."

But before Tom can say a word, Sadie comes bursting into the prison cell, out of breath. A wild, triumphant grin splits her face as she waves something in the air. It's a thin metal object, old gold in color, with fancy curlicues at the top.

"Were you looking for this?" she asks, holding the Brass Key out to me. She's so focused on me, she doesn't even notice Tom or the glowing door.

My stomach plummets into my sneakers. "What the . . . ? Where did you find that?!"

"Didn't you see the metal chest in the hall?" Sadie jerks her thumb behind her. "It was a word puzzle you had to unscramble. I lined up the tiles in the correct order and they spelled out B-L-A-C-K-W-O-O-D, and the lid popped right open."

I clench my jaw. So that stupid chest was important after all . . . and my *little sister* figured it out before me. I watch Sadie gleefully tap the base of the key against her open palm and feel the urge to rip it out of her fingers. Why can't she stick to school and stuff, and leave the games and sports to me? That's *my* specialty. Why does she have to copy everything I like?

"What were you saying the other day about me needing a miracle to beat you?" she asks, grinning, and then she finally sees Tom and almost drops the key in her shock.

"You haven't beaten me in anything, sis," I say, as calmly as I can. "You might have gotten *that* bonus, but *this* one is all mine."

Tom quirks an eyebrow at me, his lips twisting. "Is it? You won't even come through this door with me." He turns to Sadie, looking her up and down. "But maybe *you* will. Come with me, break the witch's curse, and you'll get another reward."

I grit my teeth. Now he's offering *Sadie* the bonus? I'm seconds away from flying through that door before my sister can, but then she inches closer to me. "Where does that lead to, exactly?" she demands, looking at Tom out of the corner of her eye. "What are we supposed to do once we're in? And is there a way back?"

My competitiveness dies down a little, seeing Sadie on the same wavelength as me. Bonus or not, we really don't know enough about this kid or his weird door.

"That's what I want to know," I agree. Teach him to try to hustle two Asian kids without providing all the facts. Maybe he'll give out more bonus points for being tough to push around.

But Tom doesn't look impressed with us, like I thought he would be. Instead, he looks scared and angry. "Your time's up. You've lost your chance to win the prize," he says bitterly.

Sadie glances at me in alarm. "What prize is he talking about?"

"He never really said," I tell her.

And seconds later, without so much as a see-y'all-around, Tom steps into the windy white door and it vanishes, leaving us alone in a dark dungeon cell.

CHAPTER NINE
SADIE

MONDAY IS THE FIRST OFFICIAL WEEKDAY OF SUM-
mer vacation, and it is *way* too hot to do anything other
than watch TV. My grandparents are out of town, so
Grandma isn't around to give me chores and I have
plenty of time to lounge and review what happened at
laser tag on Saturday night. I'm so busy thinking about
that weird kid Tom that I only half watch my Pixar
movie. I know it's *just* a game, and Tom is *just* a block
of code . . . so why do I keep having nightmares about
going through that glowing door in the wall and not
being able to get back out?

Mom pokes her head into the living room, iced coffee in hand. She's in a messy bun, oversize T-shirt, and
sweatpants—her favorite work-from-home outfit. "No
plans today?"

"Nope. It's a self-care day," I say, using one of her favorite phrases, and she laughs.

"I'm glad you're taking a day off from laser tag."

"Me too, actually," I admit, remembering Tom's big, bug-like eyes.

"Well, enjoy your movie. And please remind Clip to take the garbage out later." She heads back to her office, and I frown up at the ceiling, wondering what my brother is up to. He's home, which almost certainly means he's playing video games, but I don't hear any of his usual yelling or stomping. I pause my movie and head upstairs.

Clip's bedroom door is ajar. He's sprawled across his bed on his stomach, facing his phone, which is propped up against his pillows. I can see Derek's face on the screen. "This is a good idea. I can do this," my brother is saying. "I don't know why you think I can't."

"Dude, I don't think you *can't*. I just don't know if you *should*," Derek says.

I make a face, thinking they're talking about video games, until I hear Clip say, "I gotta put Sadie in her place." I freeze. "She's been, like, impossible to live with since she got the Brass Key. She brings it up every chance she gets, and it's driving me nuts."

Derek sighs. "I don't know why you guys care so

much. Laser tag's just a game, but you two have to turn it into this epic battle. Like, let it *go*."

"You don't get it, D. You're good at everything," Clip says, dropping his chin onto his folded arms. "But games and sports are all I've got. You should hear my mom and dad go on and on about how smart and perfect Sadie is . . . oh, look, she got an A just for *breathing* . . . and it's fine. It's whatever. But, like, laser tag's *my* thing, and now she wants to take over that, too."

I tense, holding my breath as I listen.

"Only my grandma thinks I'm worth anything," my brother says in a quiet voice.

"That's not true. Your parents are super proud of you . . ."

Clip ignores that and talks over him. "But it's only because I'm a boy and because Grandma's, like, super old-school. I know it's mean to like it when she yells at Sadie or makes her clean instead of me, but it's all I've got." There's a long silence. "I need to get on that *War of Gods and Men* show. I need to get on TV, and *then* that'll show 'em."

"I wish you could just play laser tag for fun, not to prove yourself," Derek says.

"I *do* have fun!" The confidence comes back into Clip's voice like it was always there. "Come on, D, I need you to have my back on this."

"I *have* your back. Always. Ever since what happened in third grade."

"I know, man," Clip says quietly.

"But I am not getting in the middle of a Chu siblings battle, so I don't know what you want me to do."

"Just support me. That's it. Sadie's won one Brass Key, and now she's number two on the leaderboard after some rando . . . Tochi O., whoever *that* is. There are still five keys left, and I'm gonna find them all. Solo. Just wait and see." Clip yawns loudly. "Anyway, did you see what Greg did with that wizard army last night? He must have leveled up without telling us . . ."

I tiptoe into my own room and close the door, clenching my jaw. I'm mad about:

1. Clip lying that I've been talking nonstop about the Brass Key. I brought it up *twice*.
2. Him pretending my win wasn't all that big a deal to him, when clearly it was.
3. The fact that he is *so* insecure that it makes me feel guilty about being good at school *and* laser tag . . . when I should just feel proud!

I ball my hands into fists. I thought finding a Brass Key would get him to respect me, so we could be a team. Instead, he's more fired up than ever to prove he's better.

Maybe it'll take more than *one* key to get him to accept that I'm as good as he is. Maybe it'll take several.

Well, if my brother wants to be rivals? We'll be rivals.

I grab my phone and call Jeremy. "I have an emergency," I say when he picks up, and I fill him in on Clip and Derek's conversation. "We need to get back to the arena *today*."

"That's so shady of Clip! He's a traitor. A Wormtongue!" Jeremy pauses. "But wait, he said he was going solo? How's he gonna play laser tag alone?"

I throw up my free hand. "I don't know, Jer! But we can't let him show us up."

"What about that freaky glowing door you mentioned? Even if we listen to that Tom character and go inside, we don't know for sure if that'll get us another key."

"We have to try. And we need to teach my dumb brother a lesson."

Jeremy exhales. "Okay. I'm in, Samwise."

"Thanks, Mithrandir," I say gratefully, ending the call. I go downstairs and knock on Mom's office door. Clip and I aren't supposed to bother her when she's working, except in an emergency. I know that means if something is on fire or someone is bleeding, but this qualifies as an emergency to me. "Mom, I'm going out with Jeremy. I'll be back for dinner, okay?"

"Where are you going?" she asks, her eyes glued to her laptop.

"Just . . . out. Maybe we'll go get ice cream or something," I fib. "I'll take my bike."

"Okay, be careful," Mom says, and I shut the door before she can ask anything else.

In the garage, I hop on my bike and pedal as fast as I can to the arena. No sooner have I arrived at the lobby than Ruth's car pulls up in front. Jeremy hops out in his *Fellowship of the Ring* T-shirt, which shows the One Ring surrounded by the faces of all nine fellowship members—a sure sign that my friend means business. I give him an impulsive hug when he comes in.

"Thanks for showing up for me."

"Always," he says, giving me a jellyfish fist bump.

As we get in line to scan in our cards, I check the digital leaderboard. It's packed with the names of mini-golf tournament winners, Skee-Ball record holders, and batting cage champions. On the laser tag list, Tochi O. has been knocked down to #5. The top spot is now occupied by someone named Tamar R., with Trisha D., Britt R., and Brian G. hot on her heels. My name's not even in the top 10 anymore.

I chew on my bottom lip. "Shoot! I wonder if all the Brass Keys are gone."

"Those people might have found other bonuses," Jeremy says reassuringly. "And look, Luellen's helping out at the scanning machine again today. We could ask her."

The blond lady is standing at the same spot she was on opening night. She's wearing the navy-blue polo that all the staff members wear. But she doesn't look as peppy and cheerful today. She looks worried, like her mind is a million miles away. I say hi to her three times, and finally wave my hand in her face to get her attention.

"Oh, hello," Luellen says robotically. "You scan your cards in, and then type your . . ."

"We're already in the system," I tell her. "We just wanted to know if there are any Brass Keys left? I found one on Saturday, but . . ."

She brightens, her pale blue eyes focusing on me. "Oh, so you're the one who found the first key, huh? Good for you, solving that word scramble."

"Sadie's amazing at word puzzles," Jeremy says proudly.

"Well, I can tell you people found three more keys yesterday, so there are still two left, hidden *somewhere* in the game. That's a total of one hundred thousand bonus points just lying around." Luellen pauses. "I shouldn't tell you which battlegrounds they're in, though."

"No, that's fine," Jeremy says. "We wouldn't want you to get in trouble with Mardella."

Luellen blinks at him for a second and then rolls her eyes. "Oh, her? She's hardly ever around." She points at the front desk, where the nice lady who talked to us on opening night—Ms. Dennis—is chatting with customers. "The COO is my boss, and she's really nice, and I don't think she'd mind if I gave the arena's first Brass Key winner a tiny hint."

I can't help grinning. "Really?"

"Really." She leans closer to us. "One of the remaining Brass Keys is up high."

Jeremy and I exchange glances. It's not much of a hint, since that could be *anywhere*—the cliffs? The galactic beanstalk in the Space Station?—but we both say, "Thanks," to be polite.

"And you'll only find it if you make sure not to lose sight of the forest for the trees," Luellen continues in a low voice. And then she smiles, straightens, and turns her back on us to help a family of six scan their cards into the system.

"The Enchanted Forest," Jeremy and I whisper gleefully to each other.

"It's the only possible battleground she could mean," he says, as we hurry in the direction of the laser tag arena. "It's not the castle or the cliffs or the lab or the swamp."

"Or the Space Station," I agree. I'm excited but also suspicious. "Is it weird that a grown-up just kind of helped us cheat? Maybe she shouldn't have mentioned the forest part."

"But her first hint was terrible. The key is up high? That gives us nothing to go on."

"It's more than what other players get." I tap my lip as we get in another line for laser tag. "But then again, she could be giving that same clue to *everyone*."

Jeremy nods. "Exactly. She's a staff member. Maybe her boss told her to feed that hint to everyone, to up the stakes."

"Plus, we could ask Tom. I bet not everyone has run into him yet," I say, cheering up a bit. "I hope he isn't only in the Haunted Castle arena."

"We saw him in the Space Station, too, remember? If he's hiding a bonus, I bet he's been coded into all of the game worlds."

We get to the front of the line and pay for our helmets, and the girl working the counter looks us over. "Only two of you today?" she asks. "You'll have to join another group. The minimum number of players in any sector is four, so we'll have to combine you. Take your pick: You can go with that group into the Mad Scientist's Lab, or that family to the Enchanted Forest."

Jeremy and I look over our options. One is a huge, rowdy cluster of people in their twenties, and then there's a family with two exhausted-looking dads and two hyperactive boys who are climbing everything in sight. As we watch, one of the boys whacks his brother over the head with his phaser, and the brother starts bawling. We smile at each other.

"We'll go with them," Jeremy says, pointing to the two dads. I know he's thinking what I'm thinking: Not only is this family going to the battleground we need, but they will 100 percent leave us alone and give us a wide berth to find the Brass Key.

Once our helmets are all on, the staff member walks us to the gate of the Enchanted Forest sector. "Elbow and kneepads on, please," she says, and the little boys stop screaming long enough to obey. After a quick run-through of the rules and an explanation of the objective (find five white apples before the other team does), the gate opens and we step into what looks more like a jungle than the unicorn-filled woodland I was picturing.

Jeremy groans. "Man, it's humid. Mardella wasn't kidding about those heat lamps."

A gust of thick, dank air hits my nostrils, and I smell

moss and bark. The family has already disappeared—I'm guessing one of their sons took off again—and Jeremy and I are alone in a peaceful clearing surrounded by dense, vine-draped trees. There's a bird chirping on a branch nearby, and when I reach out to touch it, it flies away and the leaves rustle. "This is so realistic," I say, awed, as we start walking. "So, are we looking for white apples or what?"

"Might as well. It's not like those tired dads will have the energy."

I spot a pure white apple almost immediately; the family of four must have chosen the easiest game level possible. I aim my phaser at the target on the fruit and press the button, sending the information into the program. The apple disappears. "One down, four to go!"

"Good going," Jeremy tells me, and he finds the second apple within minutes. "At this rate, we're going to end the game and get kicked out of the simulation before Tom appears."

"Let's stop apple-picking and look for him," I suggest. "Any ideas where he might be?"

Jeremy scratches his head. "Well, he told you he was trapped by a witch, right? And you and Clip found him in a dungeon. Maybe he'll be in a cage or a locked cottage or something . . ."

"Or a tower," I say, staring ahead. Through a few low-hanging vines, I see another clearing that holds a stone tower stretching to the cloudy sky. A flock of black birds is cawing loudly and circling the brick-red turrets, which are covered in a thick blanket of ivy. A single door is hanging off its hinges at the base of the tower, and I see cobwebs fluttering in the breeze. The place looks more haunted than fairy-tale. "You think he's in there?"

Jeremy shrugs, looking as nervous as I feel. "Only one way to find out. And hey," he adds, raising his eyebrows. "That's *up high*, isn't it?"

"I bet the key's up there!" I say excitedly.

We hurry over and poke our heads in to find stairs spiraling upward. The turn is so sharp, we can only see about five steps before the rest disappear. "Doesn't this remind you of the Bunker Hill Monument?" I ask. A few months ago, our history teacher, Ms. Alsberg, took us on a day trip to Boston to do the Freedom Trail and learn about the Revolutionary War. At the end of the trail, we took turns climbing the 294 steps to the top of the monument.

"Yeah, I guess it's a good thing we kind of practiced," Jeremy says, grimacing. "You'd think there would be a way to bypass stairs in a virtual simulation."

But as it turns out, Jeremy doesn't have to worry. As soon as we get onto the first few steps, they begin to slowly revolve upward and lift us like an elevator. I raise my visor slightly and the illusion vanishes to reveal that we're on a padded platform, probably with a weight sensor to let the machine know when people are standing on it.

"This is the *best*," Jeremy says, grinning.

I want to enjoy the ride up, too. Finding Tom was one of the reasons Jeremy and I came today, but I can't help feeling a little anxious. I'm not sure if we can trust him.

Suddenly, the elevator stops and we're in a small, round room at the very top of the tower. Tom is standing by the window, looking more like a hologram than ever in the bright sunlight. "Obi-Wan Kenobi, you are my only hope," I hear Jeremy say under his breath. Even though I've now seen Tom twice, my heart jumps at the sight of his soulless black eyes.

He smiles when he sees us, and it makes him look a lot nicer. "Hey, you came back!"

"We're interested in the bonus you have to offer," I tell him, deciding to play along. "Do you happen to have a Brass Key?"

Tom reaches into his pocket and pulls out a familiar-looking object: an old gold key with fancy curlicues at the top. He spins it deftly on top of his fingers. "You mean this?"

I grab Jeremy's arm and squeeze. "Yes! What do we need to do to earn that?"

"You already know," Tom says. "I showed you the door last time, and you and your brother were suspicious. Are you more willing to go through it this time around?"

"Well, we need more information first," Jeremy points out. "Like, where does the door go? Can other players see it and you, or is it just us? And why?"

"What happens when we go through the door, and can we get back out safely?" I add.

Tom sighs. "You guys ask *way* too many questions."

"You can't expect us to play the game without knowing the rules and the backstory," Jeremy says reasonably. "That's the way it works. You want us to help you? Then give us enough details to decide whether it's worth going ahead with the challenge or not."

"An extra fifty thousand bonus points isn't worth it to you?" Tom asks.

I cross my arms. "We're not going anywhere until you give us a straight answer."

"All right, *fine*." Tom takes a deep breath. "There's no witch who kidnapped me. I just made that story up so it would sound juicier. But I *do* need your help, and I *am* trapped . . . I've been stuck in here for ages. I don't know exactly how long, but I'm guessing about three years."

"In the game?" I ask, confused. "In all the game worlds?"

"They are all the same game. Just different battlegrounds."

"Okay. So what did you do to get stuck in here?"

"Nothing! I just wanted to show my friends I was a better player than them. I wanted them to know I was the best." Tom shrugs, and it's such a normal gesture that I find myself studying him more closely. For the first time, I notice that he isn't in an old-timey costume like I would expect for a character in an Enchanted Forest simulation.

He's wearing a dark blue San Francisco Giants T-shirt and jeans. "They all kept saying I was only good at laser tag because my family was telling me all of the secrets in the game. But that wasn't true. I was just *good*."

I raise an eyebrow. I feel like I could be listening to Clip talk right now.

"I wanted to prove myself, so I went in and tried to play all of the battlegrounds alone. But then I got stuck and I couldn't get back out." Tom grits his teeth. "Apparently you need someone else to play with you because a lot of the challenges are team based."

I exchange tense glances with Jeremy. "Wait a second. What do you mean, *good at laser tag*? You're a character in a game. A . . . a what do you call it?"

"NPC," Jeremy says at once. "A non-player character. They're people who are part of the game and can't be controlled by the players."

Tom laughs. "You guys don't catch on very fast, do you? I was never an NPC. I was a *player*, playing laser tag, just like you." His giant bug eyes move from me to Jeremy and back. "I was never programmed into the game. I played it . . . and then I got trapped in the code."

Jeremy takes a step backward. "No, that's not possible. That's what an NPC *would* say, to get us more into the game. Right?"

"I don't believe you," I tell Tom, getting more frustrated by the minute. "Quit messing with us and tell us how to get that Brass Key already. We want the bonus points."

A look of desperation crosses Tom's face. "Please, you guys have to believe me. I've been stuck here for so long. The only way I can escape is if I play every single battleground and win, but I can't do it by myself. Will you help me?"

Jeremy and I exchange tense glances. "Let's just pretend for a second that you're telling the truth," my friend says doubtfully. "How do we know *we* won't get stuck, too?"

"Because we'll be a team. There will be three of us to defeat all the obstacles, and I've been trapped here long enough that I know almost all the ins and outs of it," Tom says eagerly. He looks at me. "Anyway, wouldn't that impress your brother? Winning the *whole* game?"

I frown. "What do you know about my brother?"

"He didn't look too happy when you found that first Brass Key. He seemed surprised, like he thought you weren't good enough to do it." Tom tilts his head. "If you help me, I could help *you* get another Brass Key *and* you'd be doing something he never could. You'd be saving me and beating every single battleground, and that would guarantee you the number one spot on the leaderboard. That's something he's never done, right?"

My guard is up at how quickly this kid has gotten a read on me and Clip . . . but he's not wrong. If I pull this off, it would be a feat I would never, ever let my brother live down. I would be the undisputed champion of the Chu family, and a hero, too. Clip would finally respect me. "Jeremy and I need to discuss this privately. We'll let you know our decision."

Tom nods. "Okay. Whatever you need. Take the stairs back down and talk in private."

And that's exactly what we do.

"What are you thinking?" Jeremy asks, when we're back in the clearing.

"I'm thinking he's an NPC and the whole thing is just a story to immerse us in the game," I say, forcing a laugh. "Getting stuck in the game is impossible."

"Yeah," he says, but he doesn't sound very convinced.

"And if we win the whole thing, we'd get a whole lot of points for sure," I go on, pacing in front of him. "That's something Clip and Derek and all of them can't ever take away from us. That's the thing, Jer . . . They don't think we can do it. This is our chance to prove we can."

Jeremy looks up at the tower. "My gut says you're right, but something about it makes me nervous. And this sounds wild, but . . . what if he's *not* an NPC? What if he's telling the truth? Look how real this whole world is." He points to a grasshopper on a wildflower nearby. The stem wiggles as the grasshopper jumps into the grass. "Somehow, being here, it doesn't feel so impossible that someone could get stuck."

I can't help shivering, because everything he says is true. I could easily imagine us being trapped in this world, unable to get out. "If we don't do this today," I say, following his glance to the tower window, "we might lose our chance. And Clip wouldn't hesitate if it were him."

"That's a good point," Jeremy concedes. "Maybe we should . . ."

And then, suddenly, a female voice announces: "All five white apples have been located. Blue Team wins. Please raise your visors and proceed to the exit."

The simulation ends, and the forest and tower disappear. Jeremy and I find ourselves in a maze of padded mats and ropes once more. Those exhausted dads must have *really* wanted to leave if they made sure to find the apples so fast. "I guess we should go back out into the lobby and see if we can join someone else's group," I say, not bothering to hide my relief as we remove our helmets and phasers and leave them behind.

But as soon as we walk out, I catch sight of a familiar face.

"Aha!" Clip yells, pointing an accusing finger at us.

CHAPTER TEN
CLIP

"I *KNEW* YOU WERE TRYING TO STEAL ANOTHER Brass Key right from under me!" I shout at Sadie, as soon as she and Jeremy walk out. When I heard the garage door open earlier and saw my sister pedaling away like mad, I followed her . . . right to the Blackwood Gaming Arena. I cross my arms, looking with satisfaction from her stunned face to Jeremy's nervous one. "I've been out here waiting for you nerds for fifteen minutes. And judging by the leaderboard and the looks on your faces, you didn't find a key. *Big* surprise."

Sadie scowls. "Oh, stop it. We don't have time for your jerk behavior. And as for 'stealing' a key," she says, making exaggerated air quotes as she says the word *stealing*, "you're the one bragging about finding the remaining ones all by yourself. I heard you talking to Derek."

I shrug. "And I'll succeed, unlike you."

"I can't believe you fit through the doors with a head *that* big!" she roars. "What I want to know is, how are you gonna find that key if you're playing laser tag solo?"

I roll my eyes. "You've known me your whole life, and you *still* don't get what kind of skilled I am. The real question is, how would I ever find it playing laser tag with you guys?"

Jeremy looks between the two of us, quiet and worried, as Sadie's eyes narrow to slits. "How are you even a soccer player if you don't know how to play on a team?" she snaps. "It's like the Clip Chu Show, twenty-four seven . . ."

"Yeah, now you get it," I say, annoyed. She doesn't know anything about sports, let alone appreciate how tough it was for me to work my way up through the team. Learning how to be a leader is *not* easy. "I can do whatever I want to do. And I want to win, with or without you."

A few kids glance at us as they pass by in the lobby.

"You don't even care about *War of Gods and Men*," I go on. "Why are you so desperate to win those points and get on the show?"

"It's not about the stupid show! It's about proving that I'm just as good as you are." Sadie puts her hands on her hips, and I remember how she faced off against Ben Anderson on the bus. "*I'm* the one who found the very first Brass Key in the arena, after all."

I laugh. Now who's got the big head? "That was just luck, Sadie!"

My sister swells like a bullfrog, and Jeremy quickly moves between us, saying, "Guys, please . . . it's just a game. It isn't important . . ."

But Sadie ignores him. "Okay, if me finding the first Brass Key was just luck," she says, clenching her jaw, "and you're so sure you're gonna win, then why does it matter if I'm there or not? Why make secret plans to come find the remaining keys? Maybe, just maybe, you're worried not because I'll hold you back but because I'm *competition*. How about that, huh, ya big punk?"

I look my puny sister up and down. She's only a year younger, but she barely comes up to my chest. "You, competition? You think I consider *you* a rival?"

"Guys, let's calm down for a second," Jeremy tries again, putting a hand on Sadie's skinny arm. Her hands are balled into fists, like she's about to throw a punch.

I can't help laughing again, imagining her trying to hurt me. "Please, Sadie, you are *dreaming*. You're not a terrible player, I'll give you that much. But come on, you actually think you have the skills to find the last two keys before me? You don't bring much to the table."

"I think that sounds like a challenge," Sadie says, her face bright red. Her whole body is shaking with anger. "And I think I'm going to take you up on it. I'm going to find another Brass Key before you do, and I will never, ever let you forget it."

I've never seen her so furious, and for a second, I get a twinge that feels uncomfortably like guilt. A couple of years ago, we got along way better. She stuck to what she was good at, like school and orchestra, and I stuck to what *I* was good at, like soccer and laser tag. Everything was fine. And then last year, at my Lase-Zone birthday party, I figured I would just run off with my friends and leave Sadie behind . . . but she was right with me the whole time, front and center, firing lasers and climbing walls and creating battle plans. It got to the point where Iggy and Derek and Caroline were actually starting to listen to her ideas and follow her strategies. It was like seeing a whole new side of my sister . . . a side that was like *me.*

And there can only be *one* Clip Chu in this family.

"It's time you learned to respect me," I tell Sadie.

"Come on, Jer. Let's go draw up our battle plans. In *private,*" she growls, stalking away.

Jeremy gives me another worried glance. "But what about . . ."

"What about *what?*"

"What we found out today. About how Tom could maybe be a—"

Sadie holds up her hand. "No. Don't tell him anything. He doesn't deserve to know."

"How Tom could maybe be a what?" I ask Jeremy, intrigued.

He opens his mouth, but Sadie says loudly, "Tell him *nothing!* He says we don't bring anything to the table. So we're not gonna bring anything to the table." She gives me a sarcastic wave. "Good luck getting number one on the leaderboard, Clip. I hope it doesn't cost you anything . . . *valuable.*" And then, with a dramatic swing of her ponytail, she drags Jeremy out the door. I watch them unlock their bikes from the rack, arguing the whole time.

I frown, wondering what Jeremy was going to say before she stopped him. I already know what Tom is: a block of code. A cave troll guarding treasure. A nonplayer character, a plot device that immerses people in the game. I shrug. They probably just *wanted* me to think that they had unearthed something important, to punish me for telling the truth.

Because I *did* tell the truth: I'm going to win. I always win.

My phone buzzes. It's Iggy, wondering where I am. I was supposed to be at his house ten minutes ago to eat chicken wings and play some more *War of Gods and Men*. *Be right there*, I text, then take one last glance at the leaderboard and smile.

My name is going to be right at the top very soon, and my little sister will just have to accept that I was right all along.

CHAPTER ELEVEN
SADIE

"SADIE. WHAT'S WRONG?" GRANDMA ASKS, PAUS-ing in the middle of washing dishes.

I blink, and then realize I was so busy thinking about Tom and laser tag that I've been staring into my empty container of yogurt for a while. "Oh. Sorry. I was distracted."

She narrows her eyes at me. "You've been this way for two days."

It's Friday, and the house is empty except for her and me. Mom and Dad left on a mini-vacation on Wednesday, just the two of them, and Clip has been with his soccer team all week, volunteering at the local summer camp. Neither my brother nor I have played laser tag since our fight on Monday, and I'm still fuming over the awful stuff he said.

I sigh. "It's nothing, Grandma."

"See? You've been doing that all day." She imitates my sigh, drawing it out longer and more dramatically. "What's going on? Come on, you can talk to Bà ngoại."

I purse my lips. "About laser tag?"

"That game is what this is about?" She laughs, but then she sees my face and stops. "Okay, talk to me about laser tag. Why are you upset? I thought you liked it."

"I *do* like it."

Grandma dries her hands on a towel and shrugs. "Then what's wrong?"

I hesitate. She worships Clip, and I've gotten in trouble before for being less than complimentary to my saintly brother. "*Someone* is being mean to me about it. They don't think I'm as good at it as they are. And they think I can't win this bonus."

"Are you being bullied?" Grandma demands. "Who is it? Should we call the school?"

"No! I'm not being bullied. Well, not by anyone at school." I bite my lip. "It's Clip. He's being really rude, and he talks down to me."

My grandmother's face relaxes. She waves a hand, dismissing my words. "Your brother doesn't mean what he says. He's a nice, gentle, respectful boy."

"Not to me! He always acts like such a big tool!"

"Is that a bad word?" Grandma exclaims. "What did I say about using words like that?"

"*Tool* is not a bad word. And of course Clip means what he says," I say, scowling. "He thinks I hold him back when we play laser tag. And he never believes in me. He's always putting me down or laughing and making fun of me." To my horror, my eyes fill with tears. Grandma *hates* crying or any display of emotion. It embarrasses her.

"Sadie-ah, stop being so dramatic," she scolds me.

I sniffle. "He never treats his friends or Jeremy that way. Just me." The tears come faster, spilling down my cheeks. My chest feels as tight as a balloon, and I can't stop the words from pouring out, even though I know Grandma will be mad at me for saying this stuff about Clip. "Once, he . . . he even said he wished he had a brother instead of me. I don't think he would be so mean if I were his brother."

"You always think bad things about Clip! He's a great brother. I've seen you together," Grandma insists, and I shake my head miserably. It's a lost cause. When it comes to him, she will hear me, but she won't listen. "What brother spends time playing games with his sister? Not many. He is a smart, wonderful boy, and he gets excited sometimes. He didn't mean it."

"Whatever you say," I mumble, getting up to go.

"Sadie, where are you going? We're not done talking."

"What's the point, Grandma?" I ask, frustrated. "You'll deny everything I say."

She just looks at me, and her eyebrows draw together, the way they do whenever I dare talk back to her or raise my voice.

But I'm too riled up now to worry about speaking softly and calmly, the way Grandma wants me to speak. "No matter what I try to tell you about Clip, you never believe me," I say. "Maybe if I were a boy, you would believe me, since you like them so much better."

Her mouth falls open. "What did you say?"

"You love Clip more than you love me," I say, wiping away tears. "Just like you loved Uncle Jack more than you loved Mom when they were growing up. Mom told me that. It's fine, Grandma. I get it. But we don't need to talk about this right now . . ."

My grandmother is silent for a good minute, and I'm starting to wonder if she's about to blow up when she points at the kitchen table. "Sadie, sit down."

I obey at once, hearing the tone of her voice, and start to babble an apology.

"Stop. Just listen, okay?" she interrupts, and on her face is something I've never seen before: guilt. "What you said . . . it isn't true. I love you and Clip both. Equal. It hurts that you think I care less about you. Why do you think this?"

"I know it isn't true, Grandma . . ." I try to backpedal, but she shakes her head.

"Why do you think this?" she asks again.

I fiddle with the hem of my shirt. "Because you always take his side. Anytime we fight, you always think he's right. And I'm wrong or making a big deal out of stuff."

Grandma nods, like she's really listening, which surprises me.

"And you only yell at me," I go on, encouraged. "You get mad if I don't seem happy about doing chores, or if I'm not sitting up straight, or if I'm eating too little. Clip does whatever he wants, and he never has to help out at home. I get it, Grandma," I say again, when she tries to speak. "I talked to Mom about all this, and she says it was the way you were raised in Vietnam. She says you did the same thing to her and Uncle Jack."

"It *is* the way I was raised," my grandmother admits, looking down at her folded hands. "But it does not mean I love you less. I am sorry, Sadie."

I feel a twinge at how sad she looks. "No, *I'm* sorry, Grandma . . ."

"You have nothing to be sorry about. You were trying

to tell me something that made you upset, and I didn't listen. I have been trying hard to get better, but sometimes I forget. Your mom . . ." She sighs. "I made her unhappy when she was growing up. I didn't treat her and Jack the same, and she talked to me about it, too. I was mad at her at first. My own daughter, trying to tell me how to be a mother? I told her I never wanted her to bring this up again."

"What happened?"

"I thought about it some more. And I paid attention to what I was doing and saying." Grandma looks at me from the corner of her eye. "I saw that she was right. And not only that . . . I saw that it made her sad. *I* made her sad. And I don't want to do that to you, too."

I chew on the inside of my cheek as she fixes me with a stern glance.

"Do you know why I scold you?" she asks, and I shake my head. "Because you are a good girl, just like your mom. You listen to me, and you try to do better. I know you are strong and you can handle it, and Clip cannot. But this does not make it right. I will try harder. Tonight, I will scold him." She gives me a serious nod. "I will tell him to be nicer to you."

"Grandma, that's not going to help . . ."

"I will do it. But I still think he didn't mean what he

said. If Clip *knows* he is better than you, why does he have to say these things? No." Grandma leans forward. "I think he says these things because he is afraid of what you can do. You are a girl who can do *anything*."

My eyes tear up again. "Do you really mean that, Grandma?"

"Of course. And I think you should prove it to him. Don't let him stop you."

I get up and throw my arms around her, and she hugs me back tightly.

"You are my girl, Sadie," she says in my ear. "Don't ever think you are less than Clip. To me or anyone. How could you be less than him? You are my granddaughter. Now," she adds as she pulls away, done with showing so much emotion for one day. "You cheer up, okay? Grandma has work to do."

I head upstairs, feeling about a thousand pounds lighter now that I know my grandmother's on my side . . . and always has been, in her way.

I walk past my brother's room and see that his TV is still on, blasting a YouTube gaming video at top volume. That's something Grandma will never scold him for, either: leaving electronics on when he's been told so many times to turn them off if he's not home. I go in, nearly tripping on a pile of his dirty laundry, and switch it off. And that's when I catch sight of a bright orange piece of paper poking out from the mess of empty soda cans, banana peels, and video game controllers on his desk. It's the schedule for his soccer team, and there is text in almost every box for June with summer meetups and volunteering.

This week is completely full, except for today.

There's nothing scheduled for today.

I check my phone to make sure I have the right day. Clip *clearly* said this morning that he was going to be volunteering with the team all day long, the way he has been all week.

Normally, something like that wouldn't bother me. Maybe Coach Katz called together an unexpected meeting or asked the boys to come an extra day to summer camp. But for some reason there's an alarm bell going off in my head. I *know* my brother. If he had been busy all week and had Friday off, he would 1,000 percent be on his bed playing video games.

So why isn't he here?

I text Iggy. *Hey, are you with Clip at camp?*

Iggy is always on his phone, so his reply comes immediately. *Nope. No camp today.*

A suspicion begins to form in my mind. *Are you sure none of the guys are volunteering?*

Ya, I'm sure, he types back. *The camp kids are on a field trip. The team's all off today.*

Ok, thanks, I say, then I scroll through my contacts list until I find Caroline Marshall's number. I've had it in my phone ever since Clip wanted to do laser tag for his birthday last year, and she and I were in charge of helping Mom plan the party.

Is Clip at your house? I text Caroline.

It takes a minute for her to respond, but then she types back, *No.*

Have you seen him today?

No, Derek and I went out to breakfast with our dad, she replies. *Why?*

"Oh no," I whisper. I try to tell myself not to panic and quickly text Jeremy. He plays *War of Gods and Men* with some of Clip's other friends and has a few of their numbers. But within five minutes, we have confirmed that Clip is not with anyone.

Sadie? What's going on? Are you ok? Caroline texts again.

But I can't answer, because Jeremy is calling. I hit the green button.

"I think I know where Clip might be," I tell him grimly.

CHAPTER TWELVE
CLIP

I CACKLE AS I PUSH THROUGH THE DOORS OF THE Blackwood Gaming Arena. I made sure to come as soon as the place opened, and there's only a group of six other kids waiting as the staff preps the laser tag area. Two of them are high schoolers, and the rest are a bunch of six- and seven-year-olds I'm guessing are younger siblings they have to watch for the day. Two of the little girls are having a screaming match. I watch one of the teenagers break it up, feeling glad that Sadie and I are close in age and she was never that bad. And then I push her out of my thoughts, because she would be *furious* if she knew I was here.

"It's for her own good," I mutter to myself, as I pay for my helmet. The lady working the counter raises an eyebrow, and I give her a sheepish grin. "Just trying to

prove my sister wrong about something. Hey, has anyone found those last two Brass Keys?"

"Not yet," she replies. She looks kind of familiar. I
glance at her name tag, which says "Luellen B., Staff,"
and realize she was the employee who helped us scan
in on opening night. "But people have gotten close, and
maybe you will, too. Hold on, you mentioned you have
a sister?"

"Yeah. Why?"

"She's the one who found the first Brass Key, right? I
remember her. She asked the same question you did as
soon as she came in earlier this week. And you two look
a lot alike."

I try not to roll my eyes. Sadie and I look nothing
alike, but some people like to think that about Asians.
However, asking about the Brass Key *does* sound like
Sadie. "She's trying to find the last two keys before I
do, but it won't happen," I say, putting on my kneepads.

Luellen leans casually against the counter. "You guys
are competitive, huh?"

"A little," I say, and nearly snort at myself. Understate-
ment of the century.

"Well, I think you have a good chance today. Are
you by yourself?" She points to the group of kids.
"The rule is a minimum of four people per game, so

I'll need to put you with them, and they've picked the Haunted Castle. I promised them it wouldn't be *too* scary for the kids. Now," she adds, leaning forward and lowering her voice, "I'm not saying the last two keys are hidden in that battleground. But I'm not *not* saying that, either."

I raise my eyebrows. Is this woman trying to help me cheat? "Oooookay."

"Just . . . be open to any new doors you might come across. I think—"

I hold up a hand to stop her. I know it's rude to inter rupt grown-ups, but this is too much. "Thanks, but no thanks," I say, a little offended. "I don't need any clues or hints."

"It's your call," Luellen says mildly, then leads us to the gate of the Haunted Castle sector and explains the objectives. It's Capture the Flag again, and each of the teens picks two little kids for their team. They have wisely decided to separate the two girls who were fighting. One of them, a tall kid with dark brown skin and navy-rimmed glasses, glances at me.

"You need a team?" he asks.

"I'll be fine. I just kind of want to explore on my own today," I tell him.

The gates open, and the kids take off.

"Good luck," Luellen says, looking intently at me as I adjust my helmet.

I jog in without responding, annoyed that she thinks I need tips to beat my little sister. I'm a pro at this, and I don't need help from weird grown-ups. I already know that Tom's door—which she clearly meant—is where I'll find a Brass Key. Anyway, are staff members even supposed to help out the players? Shouldn't that be against the rules?

The pounding music begins and the A/C cranks on, immersing me in the game.

I run past the little kids oohing and aahing on the drawbridge. The last time I saw Tom in the Haunted Castle, we were in the dungeons. So the dungeons are where I'm gonna go. I grin and clip my phaser to my chest, heading straight for the rope ladder down to the lowest level of the castle. This will be child's play. In no time, I'm gonna be through that door and my name will hit #1 on the leaderboard. The top Chu, where he belongs.

A clap of fake thunder booms out and a couple of the little kids scream, and I chuckle as I run into the castle. I'm confident about doing this on my own today, but I do miss my friends. It would be fun to have Iggy and the twins cracking jokes beside me. But this is going to be a great story to tell them, I remind myself as I descend to the bowels of the castle.

Today, the place seems more eerie. The dungeons are mustier and darker, and two of the three torches have died out. *It's just giving the game more atmosphere*, I tell myself. I feel the bass pulsing in the floor as I make my way to the cell where I found Tom. Even with the loud music, I can hear the door creak as I open it. Something brushes my neck, like a cobweb.

"Hey, Tom?" I call into the shadows. "You here?"

There's no response.

The staff must have turned up the A/C today, because I'm shivering in my T-shirt. I frown, wondering if I picked the wrong cell, and decide to check the others. I feel the camera swiveling to follow me as I move toward the other doors, and I make a face up at it as I pass.

"That's just there for your safety," Tom says. I whirl to see him standing on the other side of the dungeon room, his eyes bottomless and dark. "I'm glad you came back. Are your sister and her friend coming down, too?"

I raise my eyebrows. "No. Not today."

"What about your other friends?"

"No, it's just me."

He tilts his head, sizing me up. "You came all by yourself?"

"Hey, what's with the third degree, man?" I ask testily. "I don't need anyone else. If you're worried about me not being able to save you, you shouldn't be. I'm the best laser tag player I know, and you're in good hands. I promise."

"You're very . . . *confident* about your skills, aren't you?" he asks, pausing just long enough to let me know he had been planning to use another word. "But here's the thing, Clip. That's your name, right? *Clip*? Some of these battlegrounds require multiple players. It's why the staff made up that rule that there have to be at least four people per game."

I sigh, annoyed with how long it's taking to manipulate this particular NPC. "Listen, I can handle multiplayer situations. One time, in *War of Gods and Men*, Iggy and Derek were sick with this cold that was going around school, so I took on a coven of witches by myself. I won *and* I got the formula for their secret potion, which saved a princess. I'm good, dude."

Tom is quiet for a moment. "You're a lot like me, you know that? I used to be obsessed with winning laser tag, too, and doing it alone to prove myself."

"Yeah, yeah, I know you have a good backstory, but I don't have the time," I say impatiently. "I'd love to get the Brass Key and, like, free you or whatever today. Can we get going? Do you have the key?"

He pulls a metal object out of his pocket. He moves

his thumb, and it doubles. Two keys. He's holding the last two Brass Keys I need. He's holding 100,000 points and my name at the top of the leaderboard. "Are you sure you want to do this?" he asks.

"Yes!" I almost shout. "Haven't you been listening to anything I've said?"

A glowing white door magically appears. It's hazy, with jagged gray lines across it. It reminds me of that test at the eye doctor, the one where you have to close one eye, look into a machine with the other, and press a button every time you see movement. The A/C, which is already up high, feels more intense in front of it. A freezing, dry wind brushes against my face.

Suddenly, I get a weird feeling in my stomach. It takes me a second to recognize that it's doubt, something I almost never feel. I never worry about winning, not with laser tag or soccer. I trust myself. I know I'll figure it out as I go. But for some reason, that cold glowing door and the bug-eyed boy watching me make me wonder if I *should* do this alone. I would feel better with Iggy and the Marshalls cheering me on, and Jeremy making his ridiculous epic fantasy speeches, and even Sadie glaring at me, determined to beat me at something, *anything*.

Every challenge I've come across so far—from the soccer field to the laser tag arena—has been with other people backing me up. Teammates protecting me or handling our opponents as I go in for the kill. Allies giving me an assist when I need it and shouting out warnings when I'm too focused on my objective to see danger.

I've always been a *leader*, and a leader needs a team.

But I've come too far now. That group of kids upstairs might capture the flag soon and end the game, and I'll miss my chance again. This is my opportunity.

"Are you coming or not?" Tom asks impatiently, and steps right through the door.

The pushy desperation in his voice rubs me the wrong way. And wait a sec . . . did he say he used to be obsessed with winning *laser tag*? I must have heard him wrong. Or maybe the NPCs in this simulation are programmed to pretend to be like us, to make the game feel more real. I think back to what Jeremy was trying to tell me on Monday, before Sadie stopped him. He had said something about how Tom could maybe be a . . . a what?

"Come *on!*" Tom says, exasperated.

And then his arm plunges out of the light and grabs my wrist. In the next second, he's yanking me right in with him. I feel this intense, powerful cold wash over my body, like I've stepped through a waterfall, only I come out the other side dry. The force of his grip nearly sends me to the ground, and I wrench my wrist away angrily.

"Dude! What's the big idea?" I demand.

"You were taking forever to come in, after all your big talk," Tom says, shrugging.

I open my mouth to argue, but then I see where we are. It's a room about the size of the dungeon. The walls, ceiling, and floor are all black, and the only light is coming from that glowing door. Every second or so, a block of green numbers skitters across one of the black surfaces, like code running over a computer screen. I see a makeshift bed that's basically a stack of padded mats, assorted cords, and wires and rope, and there's a pile of clothes, too, tossed into a corner the way I do with my dirty laundry at home.

"Where the heck are we?" I ask, stunned.

"This is called the In-Between Room," Tom says. "It lies between all of the battlegrounds of this game, and it's where I've been living all these years. It's the only section of the simulation that isn't strictly a part of the game."

My stomach twists as I stare at the padded mats, which have a folded sweatshirt with the imprint of a head on it. This is one heck of a weird backstory for a game character. It almost feels like a real person has been living here. "What do you mean, it isn't part of the game? All of this is the game. You're an NPC. You're a part of the code, and this is part of your story."

"Here, take off your helmet and kneepads and stuff. You won't need them in here, and the staff will want them back." He helps me remove my gear and, without explaining, tosses them and my phaser back out of the glowing door. "Didn't your sister tell you anything? I'm not an NPC. I ended up here because I tried to play laser tag alone and I got stuck." He plops onto the makeshift bed and gives me a bitter smile. "Just like you."

I force a laugh. "This is ridiculous. You're just testing

me to see if I'm worthy of the bonus. Right? I'm not really stuck."

"Aren't you?"

And that's when I realize the room is gradually growing darker.

I look at the glowing door, which is starting to close slowly. It's already halfway shut by the time it's taken me to have this conversation and study the In-Between Room. I dive at the door, grabbing the edge of it. But all of my strength is doing nothing to keep the opening from getting smaller and smaller with each passing second. I strain, panting as I try to slip back out.

"Help me, Tom!" I yell, but he doesn't move.

"There's no point," he says, still wearing that bitter smile. "You're in the game with me now, and there's nothing we can do to get out."

I turn my head in horror, sweating, as he shrugs at me.

"There's nothing we can do," he repeats, "except *beat the game*."

CHAPTER THIRTEEN

SADIE

"PLEASE," I BEG. "PLEASE PLAY THAT FOOTAGE again for us."

Jeremy squeezes my shoulder. "It's not going to show anything different from the last five times she played it, Sadie," he says, but the staff member—a kind-looking teenager with sparkly earrings shaped like corgis— obligingly rolls the footage again.

We're in the back office of the Blackwood Gaming Arena, staring at a bunch of computer screens. One of them shows my brother with his helmet on. His visor is down, so we can't see his eyes, but he's looking at a corner of the room and his lips are moving like he's talking to someone . . . even though the camera shows that he's alone.

"This is the Haunted Castle simulation," says the

teenager, whose name is Allison, according to her name tag. "Looks like there was a total of seven players in that particular game. If your brother came to the arena alone, he had to have been combined with another group."

I chew my lower lip as Clip continues talking to no one in the video. But from how tense he looks, I know he has to be talking to Tom. He shakes his head, like they're arguing, and then without warning, he dives into the corner of the room and disappears from view of the camera.

"Wait a second. Can you pause that image?" Jeremy asks, leaning forward.

When Allison hits the pause button, we stare at the last glimpse we have of my brother. He's leaning forward, with one arm sticking straight out in front of him.

Jeremy throws me an anxious glance. "Doesn't that look like he's being . . ."

"Dragged?" My mouth is dry. It's easy to imagine a ghostly hand gripping Clip's arm and catapulting him through an unseen door. "Allison, can you continue playing the rest of it?"

She does as I ask, and we stare at the empty screen. Even though we've now seen this footage half a dozen times, I can't help holding my breath, waiting for Clip to reappear.

But he never comes back.

"Listen, maybe your brother thought he heard someone coming," Allison suggests. "One of the other players. He might have been hugging the wall when he left the dungeons, which could be how the camera missed him."

"But why run into the corner?" I argue. "Clip's a good laser tag player. He knows the first rule is to never trap yourself." *Always leave your options open.* How many times have I heard him say that? "And even if he *did* leave the arena, he would have come home afterward or gone to one of his friends' houses."

"But no one's seen him," Jeremy agrees, his voice quiet. Ever since I called him in a panic, he's been trying to be positive and suggest that Clip went to get ice cream, or ran into a soccer buddy, or headed to GameStop before coming home. But now I can tell from his face that he's beginning to believe Tom kidnapped my brother, too.

Allison is losing patience with us at last. She gets up and pats our shoulders. "The game ended an hour ago, so it hasn't been long. And we're not missing any gear . . . all of the players' helmets and phasers were left behind in the arena. I'm sure he'll turn up. There's no way anyone can get lost on that dungeon level. It's just a bunch of little rooms."

"But I'm telling you, he went inside the game!" I say shrilly. "He's stuck inside it!"

She just looks at me without speaking.

I draw myself up to my full, not-so-impressive height. "I need to speak to Mardella . . . Ms. Blackwood. Please. We met her the night before this place opened, and she knows us."

"I'm sorry, that won't be possible."

"Please! We just need to—"

Allison shakes her head. "Ms. Blackwood is out of town. And even when she's *in* town, she hardly ever comes into the arena. Just wait and see . . . your brother will turn up soon. And now, if you guys will excuse me, it's a busy day and I need to get back to work." She glances out into the lobby, which is teeming with kids awaiting their turn for a game.

"Thanks for your help," Jeremy tells her, steering me toward the door.

In the lobby, I sink onto a bench. My chest is tight and my throat is scratchy, the way it always gets when I'm about to cry. "This is all my fault, Jer," I say softly. "I wouldn't let you tell Clip the truth about Tom, and now they're stuck in the game together. I just know it."

Jeremy checks his texts. "No one's seen him. Not Derek, not Iggy. It's not like him."

I pull out my own phone in despair. Clip hasn't responded to any of my messages, and I called Mom ten minutes ago to see if he was home. If I call again, she will *definitely* be suspicious, and how can I explain that he's vanished into a game of laser tag? I drop my head into my hands. "I can't believe what I've done. I can't believe how selfish and competitive I've been. What if . . . what if he never comes back out?"

"It's going to be okay," Jeremy says, forcing a smile. "If he's inside the game, well . . . we just have to go in there and get him, don't we? We could wait our turn, join one of these groups, and then look for Tom and try to reason with him."

"I trust that dude about as far as I can throw him, and that's, like, three inches," I say grimly. "Even when we were talking to him, he seemed so weird and desperate."

The door to the Haunted Castle sector swings open, and a bunch of laughing, chatting teenagers stream out. Jeremy and I watch them with our hearts in our mouths. I cling to the ever-shrinking but *still there* possibility that Tom is just an NPC after all—even if he's a particularly tricky and realistic one—and that it took Clip a while to figure out the bonus, but now he's about to march out and make fun of us for worrying so much. Even if he wins a Brass Key or two . . . even if his name gets up on the leaderboard and he's insufferable for the rest of our lives, I wouldn't mind it as much as I might have a couple of hours ago.

But we wait, and Clip's face isn't among the happy ones leaving the sector.

"That's it," I say angrily, wiping my arm across my runny nose. "There's no point crying. The only way to find out whether Clip's trapped is to go back in, like you said."

Jeremy nods. "I got your back. Let's do it."

I squeeze his arm gratefully, but my heart sinks at the huge line of waiting kids. "Looks like everyone came with a big group today. It'll be hard to combine us with someone else."

"They're not going to combine us with anyone else," Jeremy says, whipping out his phone again. His expression is one I know well. It's the way he looks whenever he's about to embark on a quest in *War of Gods and Men* or deliver an inspirational battle speech. "There's safety in numbers, and we need more troops to help us deal with Tom."

"You mean Iggy and the Marshalls?"

He nods.

"You think they'd believe us?" I ask doubtfully.

"I think they'd want to do something about their best

friend disappearing without a trace. I would, if *you* were in trouble. What we need," he adds, his eyes gleaming, "is a *war council*."

Half an hour later, the war council is sitting in the lobby of the Blackwood Gaming Arena, awaiting our turn to enter one of the game sectors. We told the staff that we're willing to take any simulation available, because the crowd is as thick as mosquitoes today. But even with that flexibility, there are still five or six groups ahead of us.

Caroline and Iggy believed us at once, when Jeremy and I explained the situation.

"Just wait until we find Tom," Caroline says darkly. "Nobody keeps my friends hostage."

"Clip's probably handling him fine, but if he needs an assist, I'm in," Iggy says.

Only Derek is doubtful. "Maybe it's like Allison said. Maybe Clip thought he heard a kid coming, didn't want them to find Tom and the Brass Key, and hightailed it out of there."

"But why wouldn't he text us back?" Caroline demands. "He's always on his phone."

I practically gnaw the skin off my lip as I watch the crowd in front of us. "Why hasn't this line moved? Why is everyone taking *forever* to play a stupid game of laser tag? How—"

Caroline puts an arm around me. "Stay calm, Sadie. We're gonna get him out, I promise."

"And what will we tell our parents?" I ask, my stomach wobbly with panic. "It might take another half hour or more before we even get to play a game."

"She's right." Iggy checks his watch. "It's my sister's quinceañera tomorrow, and I'm supposed to help set up for the party. My mom's already annoyed I asked for a few hours off, and there's no telling how long this will take."

Caroline looks at Derek. "Maybe we should say we're sleeping over at Clip and Sadie's house tonight. That would buy us more time."

"Dad won't like that," her brother replies. Mr. Marshall can be strict about the twins sleeping over at anyone's house, even a close friend's. "And we're right next door, so if he came and checked on us for any reason, the whole thing would fall apart."

"Just say you're sleeping over at my house," Jeremy suggests. "My parents are gone until Monday, and I can tell Ruth I'm hanging out at Sadie's house. She knows the Chus well; she won't worry or check on me."

I let out a breath. "I guess that'll work," I say, hoping Mom won't be suspicious that I'm texting on behalf of both me *and* Clip. She texts back immediately.

Clip is staying at Jer's, too?

Yeah, Jer has a new game he wants us to try, I fib, searching for a joke to throw her off the scent. *If Clip likes it, he'll prob beg you to buy it when we come home tmrw.*

It seems to work. Mom texts, *Haha, typical Clip. Okay. But you don't have your PJs?*

I grit my teeth, thinking fast. *The twins will bring extras for us to borrow. Toothbrushes, too. We didn't have time, Clip wanted to play ASAP.*

Okay, Mom says, sending three kiss-face emojis. *Call home tomorrow so Dad or I can give you a ride. Don't bother Ruth too much.*

Will do, I text back, relieved. I try not to think about what will happen if tomorrow comes and we still don't have Clip. "That's not an option," I mutter, sending back my own kiss emojis.

The others are also busy texting their parents.

"Dad's buying it," Derek says to Caroline, relieved. "He's not giving me much trouble. But he wants us home before eleven a.m. tomorrow. Think we can do it?"

"Of course we can do it!" Caroline snaps at him, seeing

the look on my face. "We're gonna get Clip out *today*. Hopefully within the hour."

"Oh, yeah, for sure," Derek says hurriedly, flashing a smile at me. "I just meant *after* we rescue Clip, maybe we'll be having so much fun that—"

"Sadie Chu's group?" a voice calls from the counter. "You're up next!"

We all sprint up to the front of the line, and I'm breathless and panicky as I watch the staff members scan their computer screens. I'm hoping for the Enchanted Forest or the Haunted Castle battlegrounds, since we've played those before and know where to find Tom quickly. For some reason, I feel like time will be of the essence. *Please let Clip be in there*, I think, my heart racing. *Please let him be safe and okay.*

"All right, you said you're fine with any available simulation, and it looks like the Deadly Cliffs is the only one open," one of the staff members says, looking at us. "Is that okay? If you want the Space Station or the Haunted Castle, you'll have to wait at least another hour."

"Yes, it's fine!" Jeremy and Iggy shout, and the staff member gives them an odd look before handing out our visors, phasers, and safety padding. Once we've all paid and suited up, he ushers us toward the entrance and explains the game objectives.

"Don't worry," Jeremy whispers to me. "We're going to find Tom, and once we do, we'll find Clip, too. And we'll get him out."

I nod and tighten my helmet, hoping against hope that he's right.

Because the alternative is too awful to consider.

CHAPTER FOURTEEN
CLIP

"WHAT DO YOU MEAN, *BEAT THE GAME?*" I STARE AT Tom. My heart's pounding in my ears, and the dark and tiny room makes me feel sick to my stomach. I take a deep breath and point at the wall where the glowing door has just disappeared. "Tom? Get me out of here."

"Even if you go back into the arena, you'll still be in the game because you came in—"

"TOM, GET ME OUT OF HERE!" I throw myself at the wall, searching desperately for the edges of the door. There *has* to be some glimmer of light from the other world . . . *my* world, where Iggy and the twins have my back, and Jeremy's got another epic long-winded speech, and even Sadie is always there when I need her. But there's no light at all.

It hits me then how stupid I've been. I've played

soccer almost every day of my life. I know how important it is to have a team. Even the strongest players can't win without someone giving them an assist, and now I've landed myself in a trap with no one to help me.

I close my eyes and lean my aching forehead against the cold concrete wall.

"Are you done freaking out yet?" Tom asks dryly. "Because I have an escape plan."

I lift my head at the word *escape*. Right now, it's the only thing I want to do. "What happened to you? Tell me everything you know," I demand.

He waves a hand over the black wall, and a glowing green keyboard appears in midair. When he starts typing, a big white screen comes into view and a woman's face peers back at us, like we're video chatting. My jaw drops when I see that it's Luellen B., the staff member who was trying to help me cheat. Her voice comes through loud and clear from unseen speakers.

"What's going on? Are you okay?" she asks Tom.

"I'm okay. How are you?" Tom asks, like they're chatting over lunch or something.

"Good! Just got back from break. I'm going to input that code override soon, and I feel sure it'll work this time. Also, I think I have some potential players for you, and I . . ." Luellen's pale blue eyes suddenly find me in the background. "Oh. You got one."

"Yeah. This is Clip."

"Well, hi there, Clip," Luellen says carefully.

Hopelessly confused, I stare at her giant face on the screen. Every wrinkle and flyaway blond hair stands out in stark resolution, and a familiar necklace gleams against her shirt: a silver chain, from which dangles a gingerbread house charm. "Wait a second," I say, pointing at it. "I know that necklace. That's Mardella's."

Luellen makes a face. "I don't want anything of hers. This is *my* candy house necklace." She glances at Tom. "You didn't tell me she was still wearing hers, Tommy."

Tommy?

"I didn't think it was important," Tom says.

My head feels like a fidget spinner. "What is going on here?" I sputter. "Who are you?"

"Luellen is my aunt," Tom tells me. "Her sister is Mardella Blackwood. My mom."

"You're the kid who died under mysterious circumstances!" I exclaim, staring at him.

"No, I didn't die," he says, crossing his arms over his San Francisco Giants T-shirt. "I've been stuck in this game for years, and my aunt's been trying to get me out."

"Is that what you mean about the code override?" I ask eagerly, turning back to the woman on the screen. "You found a way to get him out?"

"No," Tom answers for her. "I wish it was that easy.

Aunt Lu's been working on a way for me to be able to keep playing after hours, even when the arena's closed. That way, I won't be wasting every night, pacing and twiddling my thumbs and waiting for the place to open back up. The more I play, the more chances I have to get out of the game."

"Tell him the story from the beginning," Luellen advises him.

Tom takes a deep breath. "My mom, Mardella, is a genius. It was *impossible* being her kid. When she got into designing arenas, everyone wanted to be my friend so I could get them a free game. But no one believed I was good at laser tag on my own. None of my skills or strategy mattered, because they all thought Mom gave me tips."

"Didn't she?" I can't help asking.

Tom snorts. "She was too busy to even make me lunch or ask how school went. You think she'd waste time teaching me how to play?" He points at Luellen. "Aunt Lu's an award-winning game designer, too. She was the one who came up with the concept for this arena."

"Wait, what? I thought Mardella created it," I say.

Luellen shakes her head. "She stole my idea, and I only found out after I read about it in the paper. She and I never got along, you see. We competed nonstop as kids.

That's why I asked about you and *your* sister being competitive," she adds, with a half smile. "Mardella was the older, perfect one, the straight-A student. I was sporty and popular and a three-season athlete. We clashed over everything, especially when it came to which of us made our parents proudest."

I bite my lip. The Blackwoods sound a lot like the Chus.

"And it didn't stop when we grew up. We had the same dream: to become famous game designers like our parents. My mother and father were the brains behind the original versions of lots of now popular online games. *Castle of the Undead*, *Grimm Land*, *War of Gods and Men*."

"*War of Gods and Men*!" I exclaim. "My friends and I are obsessed with that game!"

Luellen gives me a faint smile. "My parents had connections at JCD Universal, which bought many of my game ideas. Five years ago, I decided to blend virtual reality with some sort of physical challenge. I knew kids would love that, and the concept for this arena was born. But Mardella stole the idea and sold it for millions to JCD. Old habits die hard," she adds bitterly.

"Dang. That's cold." Fighting? Arguing? Competing with each other? These are all Normal Sibling Activities. But stealing ideas and making tons of money off them?

Not okay. I think back to the tall woman we met outside of the arena. She had seemed so sad and nice.

"It is cold," Luellen agrees, sighing. "Her last few ideas hadn't been so successful, so she took this one from me. I didn't even know what had happened until an arena was built."

"So what did you do?" I ask.

"I demanded that Mardella give me credit, but she refused. She said *she* had put the idea in motion, so *she* should have all the credit. So to punish her, I didn't give her the whole blueprint for the prototype. I held back information." Luellen bites her lip. "She didn't care. She went ahead and built an arena on my undeveloped skeleton of an idea."

"I didn't know any of this was going on," Tom speaks up. "I just knew it was tense between them. Anyway, all I cared about was proving myself to my mom and all my friends."

"So you jumped in and tried to play the game by yourself," I say, and he nods. I can't find it in me to judge him for it. Because honestly? I would have done the same thing.

"Except I found out I can't win it alone. I got stuck somehow. I was struggling on one of the battlegrounds . . . the Deadly Cliffs. Have you played that one yet?" he asks, and I shake my head. "It's way harder than the Haunted Castle or the Enchanted Forest, and you *definitely* need more than one person to play it. I was running from a dragon—"

"Excuse me, what?"

"You and your teammates have to work together to feed a dragon and make it big so it can fly away. I couldn't feed it fast enough all by myself, so it got mad at me and started snorting fire. I *know* it was fake," Tom adds sharply, seeing my look of disbelief. "But I had been playing the game for hours and hours, and I kind of lost my grip on reality. I was . . . enmeshed."

"What does that mean? Words are Sadie's department," I say, and as soon as her name comes out of my mouth, my stomach gives a twinge. Almost like I miss her or something.

Tom gives me a look that can only be described as *scornful*. See? I know a few words of my own. "It means absorbed. Like, really into the game? Anyway, I panicked and ran."

"So what happened?" I demand.

"I saw a glowing white door. Like Aunt Lu said, this was a prototype of the game, and Mom was still beta testing. She meant for the door to be a bonus, but she hadn't fully fleshed it out yet. Anyway, I ran inside, thinking it might be a way to hide from the dragon, and I ended up in here." He angles a glance at me. "That was maybe three years ago."

"But why *you*? Why not other players?"

"We have a theory that the game somehow . . . recognizes me. Like it knows I'm related to the woman who came up with the idea for it, and the woman who put it into action. And it also knows I'm superior to other players," Tom adds, so smoothly and matter-of-factly that I feel like I could be listening to *myself* talk, and my respect for him goes up a notch or two. "So it sort of absorbed me, like a sponge, and neither Mom nor Aunt Lu can find me in the code."

Goose bumps pop up all over my arms. "That is majorly creepy."

"He's so tangled in the code that I can't risk doing anything drastic, for fear of hurting him." Luellen runs a hand over her tired face. "This is all my fault. If only I hadn't been so petty. If only I had given Mardella the whole plan, she wouldn't have recklessly built an arena off an incomplete blueprint and Tom wouldn't have gotten stuck."

"You don't know that, Aunt Lu," Tom says reassuringly. He turns back to me. "My mom came in one day and saw me tangled in the code of her game. It was almost worth it to see her so upset. She lost it. She was screaming and crying and trying everything to get me out. She kept saying she was sorry, over and over. I guess . . . I guess she did love me after all."

I can't help feeling bad for both of them.

"She confronted me," Luellen says. "She accused me of trapping Tom to punish her. I tried to calm her down, but she picked up and left without saying goodbye. I followed her across the country, trying to make up with her so we could figure this out together. But she hates me."

"How are you working at the arena, though?" I ask, puzzled. "Doesn't she know?"

She shakes her head. "Mardella's busy working on the code, too, trying to get Tom out. So she left the day-to-day operations and hiring to Naima Dennis, my boss. I dyed my hair and changed my last name so that no one would get suspicious and I could also try to help Tom."

Everything is clicking slowly together. "So that's why you gave me hints! You wanted me to go through the door to help Tom. But *wait*. You and Mardella both know how dangerous this game is. You know Tom got stuck, yet you're making a fortune getting other people to play? That's . . ." I rack my brains for a good word, but like I said, vocabulary isn't my strong point.

Tom gives a short laugh. "Don't you get it yet? My

mom opened the Blackwood Gaming Arena to find the *best* players she could. The strongest, fastest, smartest, and most competitive kids, so they could get into the game . . . and help me escape, since I can't do it alone. This is a recruiting ground for the cream of the crop."

I stare at him. "Then the arena is just a front? To capture kids and get you out?"

"No, not *capture* them," Tom says quickly. "I told you, the battlegrounds take teamwork. With the right people on my side, I can play my way out and everyone will be fine. But that's the thing. Try telling kids, 'Hey, yeah, do you want to get stuck in the code of this game with me?' No one ever wants to take the chance. But when we dangle a potential bonus in front of their noses? The *Brass Keys*? Then they start getting interested."

I feel a ripple of shame in my gut. "And that's how you got me."

"Like a fish on a hook. I was hoping you'd bring all your friends with you, but two heads are still better than one. See, I not only have to beat all six battlegrounds—I have to beat them all *consecutively*. That means back-to-back," he adds.

"I know what *consecutive* means," I snap. "So what happens if you don't?"

Tom gestures to the room around us. "You get sent

back here, to the In-Between. This place is like a default stage . . . like being inside the master computer, where your points are tallied. And if you lose, you have to start all over again from here. Right back to square one."

"I've been working day and night to try to manipulate the code," Luellen says, exhausted. "But all I could do was program a way for Tom to call up the door whenever he needs to. The only *real* way he can escape is to beat the game and win at all six of the battlegrounds." She counts them on her fingers. "The Enchanted Forest. The Haunted Castle. The Abandoned Space Station. The Deadly Cliffs. The Mad Scientist's Lab. And the Swamp of Despair."

I shake my head. "So how do you know all of this? Have you gotten close before?"

"Yeah," Tom says quietly. "A year ago, I found this group of kids. Six of them, around our age. I appeared to them like I did to you and your friends, and they agreed to help me. We played through and beat all of the battlegrounds, one by one. The kids escaped."

"So it's possible!" I say, my hope rising. "But . . . why are *you* still here?"

Tom glances at his aunt. "When you beat the last battleground, the glowing white door reappears, and this time, it takes you out of the game. It becomes a real exit. But the kids who helped me didn't turn out to be so nice. They were mad that I had gotten them trapped in the first place, so they ran through the door and . . . and left me here."

"What the . . . who would do that?" I exclaim. "That's awful. I mean, yeah, I'm pretty mad you trapped me in here with you. But that's so wrong!"

Tom lowers his head in silence.

"You've been here for *three years*," I whisper. "Is that why your eyes look like that?"

"I think I'm becoming an actual part of the game." Tom holds his hands out in front of him, and even in the dim light I can see they're shaking. "I feel it taking away bits of me every day. I don't need to eat or sleep much anymore. It's like I'm getting less human."

"I'm going to get you out if it's the last thing I do, Tommy. I swear it," Luellen vows.

The thought of spending *years* in this cramped room and popping out of a door to freak kids out with my big bug eyes is the last straw. I pace back and forth, feeling my competitive streak rear its head. It might have gotten me into this mess in the first place, but I'm going to use it to get right back out. Nothing gets me more pumped than the prospect of a challenge, a game that needs to be won, or a puzzle that has to be solved. This feels like every battle I've ever waged in *War of Gods and Men* . . . except this time, I'm playing for my literal freedom.

"Okay," I say briskly. "So we need to beat those six battlegrounds back-to-back to make that real exit appear. You say you're a good player, and I know I'm a *great* player. Between us, we at least have a shot. How does this work? How do we get started?"

Tom's face brightens at my businesslike tone. "Mom has a master computer outside that tracks all the games going on at once, and I've got one in here, too." He waves his hand over the wall beside Luellen's face, and another screen appears. It's split into six squares, each showing a different part of the arena. I see two little girls going down the twisty slide in the Space Station, and a pack of teenagers ambushing the enemy and capturing the flag in the Haunted Castle. "The security cameras in the arena feed into Mom's master computer, and also here in the In-Between. You and I have to wait for a new game to begin in one of those sectors. Once it does, we jump in and secretly complete the objectives before the actual players do."

"We're like a rogue third team," I say, scanning the screens. "A secret team."

"That's exactly right," Luellen tells me.

Tom smiles, happy that I'm catching on. "You're lucky.

I've already beaten those two worlds by myself before you got here," he says, pointing to the Enchanted Forest and the Space Station. "That means we only have four battlegrounds to conquer, but they're the hardest ones."

"So how does it work exactly? What do you do once you're in the game?"

"I wait until the players scatter throughout the arena and then choose one team to sort of 'be on.'" Tom makes quotation marks around the last two words. "Then I sneak around and complete the objectives. In the Enchanted Forest, it's collecting five white apples and taking out the enemy. Same deal in the Space Station, except you search for moon-rocks. I have to time things just right, especially when I fire at people, so they think they've been hit by the other team. And within thirty seconds of gameplay ending, I have to be back through the glowing door to the In-Between in order for the win to count. That's how this master computer tracks my victories."

It all makes a wild sort of sense. "So when the game ends, the players think it ended because of them, but it was you all along," I say, letting out a low whistle. "That sounds hard to do by yourself. But I guess when you're trapped, you gotta try."

"Exactly."

"Tom's a trooper," Luellen says, her voice fiercely proud. "He's been trying over and over again, cycling through all those battlegrounds for *years*, and he still hasn't given up once."

"Oh, I've definitely come close." There's so much sadness in Tom's voice that I can't help feeling sorry for him. "See, you'd think I would know all the ins and outs of the game after all this time. The shortcuts, the challenges . . . they should all stay the same, right? But they haven't. It started with small changes. A door I hadn't noticed. A clearing in the forest that wasn't there before. And then they got bigger and more unexpected. One time I ended up in the moat of the Haunted Castle and had to swim through it during a storm. It was awful."

"Wait, what? Who added the changes in?" I ask, shocked.

"That's the eerie part," Luellen says. "No one has. Not me, not Mardella. We're busy trying to get Tom out of a game we know well. It wouldn't make sense for us to play with the coding now. The only explanation is that the game . . . is somehow evolving. Adapting itself with each rendition, each cycle. And it's getting harder and harder for Tom to play alone."

"You're too good a designer, Aunt Lu," Tom says, with a halfhearted laugh. "I always said you were like a brilliant game sorceress or something. Anyway, Clip, I'm really sorry that you're involved now, too. And that you're stuck in here. I just . . . I want to see the sun again."

I know a real apology when I hear one. And even though I *am* annoyed that he and Luellen tricked me into the game, I want to help this poor kid out. It makes sense now why he sounded so pushy and desperate in the arena, and I can't hate on him for wanting the same thing I do: to be the best and to prove himself. "Well, like my dad says, what's done is done," I say. "And now we just have to beat this game together."

"Teammates?" he asks, sticking out his hand, and we shake on it.

"Teammates."

"Thank you, Clip," Luellen says quietly. "Thank you for helping my nephew."

"Don't thank me until we're out," I tell her, then look at Tom. "How are we gonna play without helmets and phasers? You threw mine out the door when I came in here."

"I didn't want the staff getting suspicious if your gear went missing." Tom waves me over to a low shelf, which holds a small collection of about a dozen phasers. He hands me one, and I notice it's a little different from the ones I've been using. "These are all original models my mom made ages ago. They're all we'll need to play. No helmets, because when you're in the game, virtual reality becomes reality. Everything we see will become very, *very* real."

"Like the dragon?"

"Like the dragon," he agrees. He points to the split screen showing all the battlegrounds of the arena. "So like I said, we've got four games to play. The Haunted Castle's a tough one to do solo . . . it's Capture the Flag, so you gotta be *really* sneaky and wait for a commotion near one of the flags before you steal it. You want the players to think they're the ones playing."

I nod, scanning the screen. "What about the lab and the swamp? Are they team based?"

"I designed the Mad Scientist's Lab to be a series of escape rooms," Luellen explains. "There are puzzles and riddles that you definitely can't solve single-handedly. And the Swamp of Despair also takes quite a bit of cooperation."

"So do the Deadly Cliffs," Tom says, pointing to a sector where the lights are flashing. "Speaking of which, look. A new game's about to start in that battleground. You in?"

The video feed for the Deadly Cliffs is coming from

the camera at the entrance. Tom and I watch a staff member approach, walking backward and moving his hands as he explains the rules to the new group of players. And then the players move into view.

"Hey, those are my friends!" I shout.

It's like my eyes have been starving and my friends are the food. I see Derek's and Caroline's sandy-blond heads, and Iggy towering over them with his dark hair and glasses. Jeremy's wearing his favorite Star Wars sweatshirt, the one with a Porg on the back. And in front of them all is a short, skinny girl with a long black ponytail sticking out from under her helmet. Sadie bounces nervously on the toes of her sneakers, clearly dying for the staff member to stop talking. In fact, all of my friends look worried and impatient.

I dance in place. "They're here to get me, don't you see?!"

"Yeah, I do," Tom says, staring intently at the screen. There's a thoughtful expression on his face. "You think they'll help us?"

"Of course they will!" I roar, ready to fight a dozen dragons single-handed if it means I get to see everyone again. "We'll find them and explain that they have to sit this one out, so you and I can win and get the H-E-double-hockey-sticks outta here."

"That's not what I . . . Right. They'll sit this one out."

I glance at him. I get the feeling I'm missing something important here, but there's no time to figure it out because on camera, my friends are sprinting into the Deadly Cliffs sector.

The game has begun.

"Come on, let's go!" I urge Tom.

He waves his hand over the computer screen, and it disappears. In its place is a white light that grows and grows until it takes the shape of that familiar glowing door.

"Good luck, boys," Luellen says.

Tom yanks the door open, and then we're racing through it and back into the arena.

THE DEADLY CLIFFS SIMULATION IS EVEN MORE realistic than the Haunted Castle or the Space Station. As soon as we snap our visors into place, we find ourselves halfway up a mountain of bloodred rock. The sun beats down from a hot blue sky, and enormous black birds swoop above us, piercing our eardrums with their shrill cries. I breathe in the smell of chalky earth and a musty, uncomfortably warm wind and cough a couple of times, already parched from the dry desert air.

"Okay, so obviously we're looking for Clip, but also a baby dragon?" Iggy asks.

"And some roc's eggs, to feed the dragon so it can grow its wings and fly away." Caroline scratches her head. "Whatever a *roc* is."

"A huge, mythical bird of prey," Jeremy says at once. "Sinbad the Sailor encountered one on his second voyage. He rode it off a deserted island into a valley of giant snakes."

"Who's Sinbad the Sailor?" Derek asks, puzzled.

"And who would want to go into a valley of giant snakes?" Iggy adds.

"Never mind," I interrupt, as Jeremy begins to explain. Normally, I love his lectures because they're full of interesting info, but not while my brother is being held hostage. "Let's go find what we need to, but don't end the game before we can get Clip."

Everyone nods, and then stares at me. I realize suddenly that they're waiting for *me* to lead the group. It's the weirdest feeling, because no *way* would my brother let that happen if he were here. *But he's not here, and he might never be again*, I think, before I can stop myself.

Quickly, I turn and head up the treacherous path, knowing the prickling in my eyes has nothing to do with the dry air. Everyone follows behind me, stumbling on the rocky terrain. The trail up the mountain is littered with sharp stones that move under our feet, threatening to twist our ankles, and bulky fallen tree branches with dry, withered leaves.

"Man, it's hot. I wish I hadn't worn a sweatshirt,"

Jeremy moans, huffing and puffing behind me. "I have a feeling we'll come across the dragon soon."

"Why? Won't it be at the top?" Derek asks.

"Nah. They like caves. They're always holing up in little nooks and crannies, hoarding treasure. I'm thinking if we see a cave, we should go in. Once we locate the dragon, the roc's nest shouldn't be far, and then we can focus on Clip," Jeremy adds, patting me on the back.

"I hope he isn't here," I mutter. "I hope he's getting ice cream and just being a jerk and not answering our texts."

"You and me both," Iggy agrees. "I hope . . . Ugh, what is that *smell*?"

I smell it, too: a pungent, thick odor that's like a combination of a middle school gym locker, the darkest corners of Clip's room, and the trash can at high noon.

"Wow, that is ripe," Caroline says, waving her hand in front of her nose.

Only Jeremy looks happy. "We're definitely close to the dragon. The ones in the Ninety-Nine Kingdoms of Windermere series—remember those books, Sadie?—always smelled awful, too. It's because of the sulfurous gases they release . . ."

"Please, Jer, can we not talk about dragon farts?" Derek asks, looking pained.

"No, no, it's from the fire they breathe," Jeremy explains, but he doesn't get to continue, because a deafening roar shakes the ground. Rocks dislodge from the mountainside, roll across the dirt, and bounce off the cliff. I watch a boulder career into the valley below, thousands of feet beneath us, and feel nauseous seeing how high up we seem to be.

The path curves sharply to the right, taking us to a sort of landing on the mountainside.

The disgusting smell is wafting from a huge opening in the rock wall ahead of us. As we peer in, a huge pair of slitted golden eyes suddenly blinks out from the darkness. I grab Jeremy's arm, and Iggy trips over a fallen branch in his shock.

"Oh my god," Derek utters, as the monster reveals itself to us in its full glory.

The dragon is the size of two SUVs stacked on top of each other. It has four muscular legs, greenish-gray scales, and a pair of tiny red wings on either side of its thick body. It looks a lot like Smaug from the Hobbit movies, and I can tell from the worship in Jeremy's eyes that this fact has not escaped his notice, either. The creature stomps out slowly, rattling the earth with each lumbering step as it watches us with its mean reptilian eyes. The stench and the heat intensify as it stops about ten feet away, its ugly head swinging to look at each of us.

"That's a *baby*?" Iggy tries to lift his visor to see what it really is, but Jeremy stops him.

"Don't! You'll spoil the magic."

"Dang, what magic? That's one ugly beast, and if it mauls me—"

The dragon's massive jaws part in insulted rage. It releases another earth-shaking roar that I can feel vibrating in my bones. And even though I *know* it's not real, I can't help swallowing hard as the monster growls, deep inside its chest.

"Hey, hey, it's okay," Jeremy tells the dragon, in what he clearly thinks is a gentle, soothing voice. It stops growling and regards him with a single slitted eye. "Don't listen to him. Can you show us where the roc's nest is? We'll get some eggs for you to eat."

"Yeah, we'll feed you," Derek chimes in, and the dragon's head swings to look at him. "We want to help you fly far, far away from us . . . ouch!" Caroline jabs his ribs with an elbow, because the dragon's eyes have narrowed, like it's getting mad again.

"Guys, I think it's *hangry*," Iggy says in a low voice. "Maybe we should just go."

"The roc's nest must be nearby," I say. Still clutching Jeremy's arm, I shuffle as close to the edge of the cliff as

I dare, skirting the furious-looking dragon. Its head turns slowly, eyes never leaving us, as everyone moves up the path in a terrified cluster.

And then, without warning, the monster stands up on its hind legs and begins to follow us, quicker than I could have imagined a creature of its size would be.

"Oh my god!" Derek yelps, seizing Caroline.

"Calm down, you guys! Chill out!" Jeremy hisses. "I don't think it's chasing us. It just wants to come along. Move slowly or you'll look like prey!"

But the Marshall twins aren't listening. They are *panicking*. They push past me and Jeremy and sprint up the steep incline, sending back clouds of smoke. Their fear has taken hold of Iggy, who grabs Jeremy and me by the scruffs of our necks with his huge hands and propels us upward. Seeing us speed up, the dragon has also quickened its steps. Every time its enormous body hits the ground, it causes a mini-earthquake, making it even harder to ascend the mountain.

"Derek! Caroline!" I yell, as they disappear around a corner.

And then Caroline screams.

"Sounds like she found the roc?" Jeremy asks hopefully.

But when we tear around the corner with the dragon in hot pursuit, we don't see a giant predatory bird; we see the Marshalls hugging a very familiar figure.

"Clip!" I shriek, and my brother untangles himself from the twins and actually hugs me. I don't think he has *ever* done that of his own free will. For some reason, he's not wearing a helmet or a vest. I point to my own gear. "Are you okay? Where's your . . . ?"

"No time to explain," Clip shouts, so everyone can hear him over the thundering steps of the dragon. "Roc's nest is this way!"

He charges up the mountain at a pace only Derek and Iggy can match. Normally, that would annoy me, but today I'm just thankful he's here and he's okay. Jeremy, Caroline, and I huff and puff after them and find ourselves on yet another landing in the cliffside.

The nest in front of us is *gargantuan*. It's the size of a swimming pool and made entirely from tree branches and withered leaves. There's a powerful smell of rust and moss from it, which I will gladly take over the stench of the dragon. In the center is a clutch of gigantic sky-blue eggs with navy veins jutting over their shells. The veins form a bull's-eye on the front of each egg—a strike zone for our phasers. I peek at Jeremy, to make sure he's not looking at me, and lift my visor. I'm dying to know what we're really looking at.

"Balls!" I can't help choking out.

Clip looks at me, shocked. "Sadie! Watch your language, please."

"No, stupid! It's a ball pit!" I snap my visor back down, ignoring Jeremy's look of disapproval, and plunge into the nest. The "tree trunks" move easily around my legs. "The whole nest is made up of little plastic balls, and the eggs in the middle are giant beach balls."

Clip throws himself into the ball pit with me. His arm jostles mine as he pushes to get to the eggs first, but I'm smaller and faster and lay hands on them before he does. Still, he has to win at *something*, so he yanks out his phaser and shoots the bull's-eye on the egg I'm holding.

"Hey! This one was mine!" I yell.

"You have to hit the target first before you pick up the egg," he says bossily, then snatches it out of my arms and turns away.

The dragon is mere feet from us, its furious yellow eyes zeroing in on the item in my brother's hands. Smoke begins to stream out of its nostrils.

"You want this, big boy?" Clip shouts. He executes a perfect drop-kick that sends the egg right into the dragon's mouth. The monster's eyes close for a second, the way mine do when I'm eating Grandma's pho, and then they open again, looking even hungrier.

"Goooooooooooooooal!" yell the Marshall twins, dancing around.

"My turn!" Iggy fires his phaser at another egg and

launches it into the creature's mouth. "Yeah, you like that, don't you?"

A thought occurs to me. I turn to Jeremy, who has been cheering and clapping. "If the nest was here the whole time, why didn't the dragon just come up and get the eggs itself?" I ask.

In the next five seconds, two things appear: the answer to my question, and Tom.

The boy's bug eyes are wider than ever as he points frantically at the sky, where a monstrous shadow has just blocked out the sun. "Guys!" he yells. "Watch out!"

"Yep," Jeremy says weakly. "That's the roc."

"Get low!" Clip yells, yanking Jeremy and me down.

The roc is a black bird of epic proportions. It lowers itself about a foot over the nest, its wicked wings sending a gust of hot, dusty air upon us. Its eyes are bright red with a black pinprick in the center, and they roll with fury at the sight

of us rob-
bing its nest.
The poisonously
orange beak opens and
emits a high-pitched shriek
that sends everyone's hands flying to their ears. In
response, the dragon roars with terror and attempts
to flap its own tiny red wings. They lift its bulk about
three feet off the ground, but clearly aren't strong
enough yet.

"It needs to eat more!" Derek shouts, watching the
dragon struggle to get away.

Iggy, who is closest to the eggs, fires a laser at another
bull's-eye. But before he can grab the egg, the roc's sharp,
evil-looking talons descend and block it from view. It

shrieks with anger, its wings beating harder than ever, and Iggy rolls hastily away from its feet.

"I think we probably need to hit the bird, too!" Tom yells, looking more like a hologram than ever with the sun shining through him. Neither he nor Clip are wearing helmets, but they're holding phasers like ours, and he points his upward. "Yup, I was right! See how there's a bull's-eye on the underside of the roc? We gotta hit it there!"

He directs his laser toward the target and fires. The roc blinks its bright red eyes and rears its head back in another ear-splitting scream.

"Come on, let's help!" Caroline shouts, climbing to her feet. Derek, Iggy, and Jeremy all hurry after her, phasers at the ready, and I'm about to go, too, when Clip grabs me.

"Let them handle it! Someone's got to feed the dragon," he says.

It's proof of the danger we're in that I neither argue nor point out how my brother needs me to help him win, *again*. We plunge toward the six remaining eggs, which are fair game now that the roc is busy swooping around to avoid the phasers striking it.

I aim my phaser at the nearest one, hitting the bull's-eye with a *ping!* before chucking it at the dragon's mouth. No sooner has the beast swallowed the egg than Clip's launched another one. I lob the third egg, and my brother takes care of the fourth. Only two more to go.

"Hurry up, you guys!" Derek screams. He and the others throw themselves to the ground as the roc lunges furiously downward, talons missing them by bare inches.

Tom, however, is still on his feet, firing at the bird like it's his last chance at freedom. And maybe it is. "Keep going, guys! You're doing great!" he yells at me and Clip. "I got this!"

I fire at the fifth egg and toss it into the dragon's mouth. The creature's wings are lifting it higher and higher every minute, and soon they will be strong enough to carry it away. Hastily, I fumble for the sixth and last egg, but my brother shoves my hand aside.

"My turn!" he shouts, ignoring my scowl. Even while facing down monsters, he always has to have the victory shot. A smug grin crosses his face as he picks up the final egg, releases it, and drop-kicks it toward the dragon. But in his hurry, he overshoots.

The egg angles to one side and smacks the dragon on its left cheek.

"No!" Jeremy cries, as the egg bounces off and heads straight for the edge of the cliff.

There's no time to think. I throw myself out of the nest and dive toward the escaping egg, seizing it just as it's about to fall off the mountainside. Panting, I fling it into the dragon's mouth with all my strength. Instantly, the monster begins to ascend, its red wings—still small, but now more powerful—beating hard against the hot air and lifting it off the mountain.

"Guys! Get over here!" Tom yells. He's still shooting at the roc, which is weakening, but the glowing white door has reappeared beside him. "Clip, get everybody inside and get their gear off! Helmets, kneepads, everything. Throw it back out!"

Clip hesitates.

"What does he mean, get us inside?" I shout, over the commotion of the bird's wings.

"There's no time to lose, Clip!" Tom yells over his shoulder. The roc swoops, and he flattens himself on the ground, still screaming at my brother. "This is our one chance to have a big team! And the victory will count as *theirs* if you don't do as I say! Not yours and mine!"

Clip looks at me. "Do you want to help me escape the game?" he asks, speaking loudly so I can hear him over the shouts of the others. The roc swipes at them with its razor talons, then turns its bright red eyes upon Clip and me and heads straight for us.

I scream and duck as the bird nose-dives toward me. "Yes! Duh!"

"No matter what?" Clip yells.

"Yes! And so does everyone else! That's why we came in after you, dummy!"

"Okay, then, everyone, get inside the door! Take off your vests and helmets and throw 'em back out! I'll explain later!" Clip hauls me to my feet and sticks out his long arms, sweeping us all toward the glowing white light. "This is how Tom and I win the game. We have to win all the battlegrounds before it will let us escape!"

"But if you're stuck in the game, then won't *we* also be . . ." Iggy begins, but there's no time to finish the question. We're racing through the door into a weird, dark room, the opposite of what I had imagined a sparkly game bonus to be. One by one, everyone tears off their vests and kneepads and helmets, tossing them back out the door.

Clip jumps in after us. "Throw your phasers out, too," he says, snatching mine away without asking and chucking it back into the arena.

"But why?" Caroline protests.

"Just do it," Derek urges her, seeing the frantic look on Clip's face.

Everyone is now stripped of their gear as Tom puts one foot inside the door and fires a parting shot at the roc. The bird throws its head back and falls in an epic spiral toward the nest, but we don't get to see the impact because Tom rushes in with us and closes the door, enveloping us in almost total darkness. We can barely see our surroundings. Green numbers skitter over the black walls every few seconds, like code inside a computer.

There's a silence punctuated only by the sound of everybody breathing hard, winded from our fight with the monsters. Tom leans against the wall, his eyes gleaming with triumph.

"Um, Clip?" I ask. "Where the heck are we?"

CHAPTER SIXTEEN
CLIP

EVERYONE IS DEAD SILENT AS TOM EXPLAINS WHAT he told me before: how Mardella is his mom, how he got stuck and his aunt Luellen is trying to help him, and how he and I have to beat all of the six battlegrounds to escape. I jump in every now and then to be helpful, but even after we're done telling them all the details, my sister and our friends don't say a word.

Until they all start talking at once.

Or maybe the right word is *yelling*.

"Wait a sec, so we're stuck in the game now, too?" Sadie shouts.

"You should have told us before!" Iggy protests.

"What do you mean we can't get out?" Jeremy cries.

"Let me out of this creepy room!" Derek yelps, at the same time Caroline is banging on the wall where the door was and groaning, "Oh my god, oh my god, this is my nightmare . . ."

And none of their eyes are on Tom. They're on me, and they're accusing, and Sadie's face is the scariest one to behold. "Look, guys, I'm sorry. But I had no idea you had to come through this door with us until the last minute. *Tom* never said anything about that," I add, trying to turn their anger on the main guy responsible for all this.

"I told you *we* have to win the victory in order for it to count. You and me. Not the players," Tom says in a know-it-all voice that makes me want to punch him.

"But *we* could have gone in," I say, confused. "Why did my friends need to come, too?"

Sadie growls at me. "We didn't need to, dummy! Remember what he said? *This is our one chance to have a big team?* The more people on your side, the more likely he'll get out!"

"Wait, so this little twerp is putting us all at risk on the off chance he can escape?" Iggy asks, glaring at Tom. In the dark, his height and bulk are intimidating.

"If we win, we all win," Tom says, holding his hands out like he's trying to calm a pack of wolves. "You want Clip to escape, don't you? Think of this as you making a sacrifice for *him*. Helping *him* out."

Sadie snorts. "You talk like a corrupt politician. You dragged us in here to help *you*."

"But if helping me helps you, what's the difference?" Tom asks, taking a step backward as my friends start yelling again. "You guys think I like tricking other kids into the game? I hate it. But I have no choice! For the past three years, Aunt Lu and I have searched for a group of players worthy enough, and *brave* enough, to help me. And like I told Clip, I found some a couple of years ago. But when we won the whole game, they escaped and left me here."

The anger in the room dies a bit. Sadie and Jeremy exchange glances.

"Why did they do that?" Derek asks, shocked.

"Because they were mad at me for trapping them. Just like you guys." Tom tells them what he told me: how when the real exit appeared, the kids ran out and shut the door on him.

Jeremy frowns. "That's awful. But none of us would do that if we end up winning."

"*When* we end up winning," Sadie corrects him, then scowls at Tom. "So what about our group makes you think we can help you? Why us?"

"Look." Tom pulls up the computer screen again, the one that shows all six sectors of the arena. We watch kids firing phasers, climbing ladders, and swimming through ball pits, all of them having the time of their lives. "Aunt Lu and I monitor these feeds obsessively. No one has ever impressed us as much as you. You're *way* better than that group that left me. You all bring something different to the table. Clip's a leader, and you and your friend . . ."

"Jeremy," Sadie says, crossing her arms.

"Right. You guys are the brains. And you two are fast," Tom says, pointing to the twins, "and you, the big guy, you're strong. Put together, you make an amazing team. And I just . . . I knew you'd hate me for dragging you into this. I mean, *I* would hate me." He stares down at the floor, and his voice gets all quiet. "But I hoped you'd want to help me, too."

Caroline bites her lip. "You've been living in here? In this tiny room?"

"Yeah." Tom sinks down against the wall, looking exhausted and miserable. "I'm so sick of this. Sick of hiding Aunt Lu from Mom and being stuck in the middle of their grown-up mess, when *they* should be handling it. Sick of waking up every day to play the same game over and over, but never getting better at it because it keeps changing. And at night, when the arena closes, I have to wait and wait until it opens again. It's torture."

"But your aunt's working on the code for that, right?" I say, and he gives a tired nod. "She's trying to figure out a way for you to keep playing at night, too."

Iggy shifts his weight from one foot to the other. "So, what you said about the game evolving? Like, adapting on its own? What did you mean?"

"I've played the Deadly Cliffs hundreds of times, and I've never had to fight the roc. It was only ever a distraction before. This is the first time firing at the actual bird has been an objective." Tom lets out a long breath. "And the last time I played the Enchanted Forest, there was a new tree maze I got stuck in for hours. The game's always one step ahead of me."

Jeremy shivers. "But how is it possible if your mom and your aunt aren't coding new challenges in? How can a game change by itself?"

"How can a game trap a kid for years?" Tom asks with a bitter smile. He looks around at all of us. "Look, guys, we're all a team now. I beat the Enchanted Forest and the Space Station by myself, and you all helped me with the Deadly Cliffs. All we have left are the Haunted Castle, the Mad Scientist's Lab, and the Swamp of Despair. Once we beat those, we're out."

I look at Iggy and the twins, and I can tell they're starting to feel as bad for Tom as I do.

Sadie and Jeremy still look wary, though. "So here's a question for you," my sister says to Tom, putting her hands on her hips. "How are we even gonna play the game without helmets and phasers and stuff? Why did you make us throw everything back out?"

"So the staff doesn't get suspicious when five sets of gear go missing," Tom says.

Jeremy raises his eyebrows. "What about five *kids* going missing? Won't they get suspicious about a whole group that just never left the arena?"

"Eventually, yes. But returning your stuff buys us time. They'll find the right number of helmets and phasers left behind, and maybe they'll think that they somehow missed all of you leaving. Anyway, I have phasers in here." Tom points to the dusty shelf.

"Oh yeah," Sadie says, frowning at me. "How did you guys see the roc and the dragon and the nest and everything without helmets?"

I shiver. "Because virtual reality became reality. I didn't need the visor to see everything. It was like . . . like I was actually there, and the dragon and the roc were, too. A couple of times, I forgot I wasn't wearing a helmet and I tried to lift it. But I couldn't."

"Because you're in the game," Jeremy says, and I nod miserably.

There's a long, horrified silence.

Sadie whirls on Tom. "Okay, fine. So let's say we play. If we're this so-called secret team and we need to win without the real players noticing, how the heck are we going to do it on these last three games? It's gonna be kind of hard to hide *seven* extra people."

Tom nods. "The castle will be tricky. We'll have to hide around the arena and divide into groups: one to take out the opposing team, and one to capture the flag. But the swamp and the lab will be easier, 'cause all the players have to split up and they'll be less likely to see us." He holds up his hands again. "Look, I know you don't trust me. But I also know we can do this together."

"You should have told us who you were from the beginning," Sadie snaps. "From the very first time I saw you in the Space Station. You should have told us you're Mardella's kid."

"But if I had, you might not have wanted to help me," Tom protests, then sees the look on her face and sighs. "I'm sorry I didn't tell you."

"Sadie's right. Anything else you want to reveal now?" Jeremy asks.

"Come on, guys, leave him alone," I say, surprising even myself. I never thought I would be defending Tom, but honestly? The kid's been through enough. "Bottom line is, we're stuck in here now and we gotta find a way out. So let's stop wasting time and play."

Iggy and Derek are still focused on the computer screen, mesmerized. "Look, the current game is ending in the Haunted Castle," Iggy says, pointing. We all watch the lights flashing in that sector. A group of eight or nine kids leaves, and then several staff members come in to sweep the area, collecting the players' gear and making sure everything is in order.

"Should we do that one next?" Caroline asks, glancing at me.

"Might as well. It's one of the battlegrounds we need," I say, and catch sight of Sadie's and Jeremy's faces. They look scared and doubtful, and that's when the weight of it all starts settling on my shoulders. The fact that my sister and friends are trapped here because of me? It doesn't sit well. "Look, guys, we've played this sector before. Even if it changes somehow," I add, as Tom gets to his feet, "at least we've been there already. There are seven of us. We got this, okay?"

"We might as well try," Jeremy says tentatively.

"Do we have a choice?" Sadie asks, glaring at Tom.

"Okay," I say. "So, we have to pick a team to 'be on.' Executive decision: We're on the purple team. So that means we need to steal the green team's flag and also take out all of the green players by firing at them three times each."

"Sadie and I are the fastest ones," Caroline says. "So maybe you should split us up."

"And Sadie and I work well together," Jeremy adds.

Iggy flexes his arms. "I want attack team."

"Okay. Attack team will be Iggy, Derek, and Caroline," I say, pointing at each of them in turn. "And the flag capture team will be me, Sadie, Jeremy, and Tom."

Sadie and Jeremy move to stand close to me. "Where should we meet when we're done?" my sister asks suspiciously, pointing at Tom. "*You're* in control of that weird door, right? The one that leads back here? How do we know you won't lock one of us out or something?"

"Why would he do that, Sadie?" I ask, annoyed.

She throws her hands up. "I don't know, Clip! This kid literally trapped us in a game with him. How am I supposed to understand how he ticks?"

"Our lives are on the line and you're busy picking him apart."

"Oh, sorry for being thorough!" Sadie says sarcastically. "A good laser tag player should know all the details before jumping in and—"

"A good laser tag player relies on instinct, not overthinking," I point out.

"Yeah, yeah, because every time you hear 'good laser tag player,' you think it's you!"

"Guys, come on!" Caroline groans, pushing us apart. "I know you two like to compete over everything, including breathing air, but, like . . . chill out!"

"*Seriously*," Iggy agrees. "Maybe they shouldn't be on the same team."

Sadie scowls. "It's fine. We don't need to be separated like two toddlers in time-out."

"Well, you're acting like it," I hear Iggy mutter, but I pretend not to hear.

While we were arguing, Tom has been collecting phasers from the dusty shelf. He starts handing them out. "To answer Sadie's question, we need to get back to the In-Between when we're done. *All* of us," Tom says, making eye contact with my sister. "Only then will we clinch the victory, because this room is where the master computer tracks our wins. So I promise I won't be shutting anyone out." He looks at Iggy and the Marshall twins. "Attack team, when you're done taking out the other team, you'll have to come meet us in the green flag tower."

"Got it," Derek says, and Caroline and Iggy nod their agreement.

Everyone looks worried, but even Sadie accepts her

phaser without further argument. It's not like any of us really have a choice. On the monitor, a new group of players appears in the Haunted Castle: two guys and two girls, maybe sixteen or seventeen years old.

"There are only four of them," Derek says, looking relieved. "That shouldn't be so hard."

"Doesn't this seem kind of unfair, though?" Jeremy asks. "There are seven of us, plus the two on the purple team. That's nine people against the two on the green team."

Tom shrugs as the glowing white door reappears. "Tough luck for them, but then again, *they're* not playing for their lives. Are you all ready? On your mark, get set . . ."

He doesn't say the word *go*, but I know we're all thinking it as he plunges through the white door. And bam! We're back at the Haunted Castle. This time, without helmets, it looks even more incredibly, scarily *real*. Loud, intense music with a heavy bass vibrates in the ground beneath our feet. Two ragged flags, one green and one purple, wave against a moonless night sky in the freezing wind. Torches flicker, illuminating the outline of a great stone castle, and we hear the sound of rushing water from the raging moat and its white-capped waves. On the drawbridge are the four teens, strolling toward the entrance like they have all the time in the world.

"What are they doing?" Iggy scoffs. "This isn't a time for sightseeing!"

"Maybe they just want to explore," Derek suggests.

Finally, when the teens disappear, we all nod at each other. Iggy and the Marshalls sprint off in pursuit of the green team, and then Tom, Jeremy, Sadie, and I follow behind.

"Is it me or did they turn up the A/C even more?" my sister asks, shivering.

"It does feel a lot colder. And there's a burning smell, too," Jeremy says with an appreciative sniff. "Very authentic. Like rotten wood and moss and peat."

"What the heck is peat?" I ask.

But he doesn't answer, because he, Sadie, and Tom are all staring open-mouthed at the castle courtyard. When I see it, my jaw drops, too. Between the drawbridge and the castle is now an enormous hedge maze, its walls of tangled, sharp-looking green briars soaring ten feet into the air. The wind ruffles my T-shirt, bringing with it the smell of mossy water and damp earth.

"What is this? There's never been a maze before," Sadie says worriedly.

Tom's face is pale and grim. "See what I mean? This is what I was saying about the game changing. I've played this sector a zillion times and I've never seen this here."

"So what else is gonna happen?" my sister demands. "Will we have to fight goblins?"

"I guess we'll find out," Tom says.

Sadie huffs out a breath, but she and Jeremy stick close behind as Tom and I sprint into the hedge maze. The briar walls seem to muffle the sound of the wind and the water, and I can hear our footsteps and panting under the loud pounding bass of the music. It's dark, with only a couple of flickering torches at every corner where walls meet. Again, I'm desperate to lift up my visor and see what I'm *really* looking at . . . but of course I can't. We jog down long passages and around corners for a while before I hear Sadie calling me.

"Hold on, Clip," she says, looking back at Jeremy. "Let's catch our breath for a sec."

Jeremy leans against a wall, breathing hard. "Doesn't this remind you," he says cheerfully to Sadie, panting, "of that book series, A Song of Moss and Sea? Remember how Peter, the witch hunter, had to collect the eight rubies of invincibility, and . . ."

A shadow dances over the nearest hedge.

"Quiet!" Tom whispers, and I yank my sister and Jeremy into a dark corner formed by the joining of two walls. We keep still and quiet as footsteps approach, and then . . .

"Oh, it's just you guys," I say, relieved, as Iggy, Derek, and Caroline come into view.

"What's wrong? Why are you coming back out?" Tom asks.

"We're coming back out?" Derek groans, glaring at his sister and Iggy. "I *told* you guys we should have turned left instead of right. We must have gone in a circle."

Caroline grits her teeth. "Now we'll have a heck of a time catching up to the green team."

"Let's just retrace your steps," Tom suggests. "No sweat. Come on."

He and the Marshall twins take the lead, swerving our group to the left and then to the right. I find myself jogging next to Iggy.

"Hey, man," he says. "I know you feel guilty about pulling us in here. But, like, we would have insisted on coming in anyway, even if you hadn't. Especially Sadie."

I shake my head. "I don't know about *especially Sadie*."

"Why not? She's your sister. Look at Derek and Caroline—they'd do anything for each other."

"Yeah, but they're different. They . . ." I look for the right words as we jog, but it's hard to explain. "They're the opposite of me and Sadie. Like, *you* know what I'm talking about. They didn't grow up with our background."

Iggy laughs. "I do know."

"Their parents and grandparents don't treat them like a spectator sport . . . like everything they do can earn or lose them points. Like life is a whole contest." I sigh as we round a corner. "They don't know what it's like to have to come out on top every time, or else your parents will think you're the useless, stupid Chu your whole life."

"You're not useless or stupid. Nobody in your family thinks that, dude."

"Except Sadie," I mumble.

Iggy looks at me. "Is that what this is about? You just want her to look up to you?"

I grip my phaser, trying to squash down all the touchy-feely emotions threatening to burst to the surface. "I don't want to talk about this right now," I say gruffly.

He shrugs. "That's cool. Anyway, I think those teens are two couples," he adds, changing the subject with a hint of disgust. "One guy and girl made out for *forever* in a corner, but luckily they were our team, the purple team. So we followed the other two, who were holding hands like they were in a park or something. And then Caroline tripped, and when Derek and I helped her, we lost them."

"That's okay," I say, waving a hand. "We haven't been playing laser tag for *years* for nothing. You'll find them, and they should be easy to take out."

"It's not them I'm worried about. It's the arena."

Ahead of us, Derek is waving excitedly and pointing at a flickering torch on the hedge wall. "I think this is the intersection where we took the wrong turn. See how this light is brighter than the others? That's how I remember. We should go left this time."

And then we're out of the hedge maze, and the castle doors are right in front of us.

"Way to go, guys!" I say. "Okay. Back to the original plan!"

Derek, Caroline, and Iggy hurry off, and then my team and I follow, angling toward the east tower, where the green flag is waving. The interior of the castle looks just like I remember it, including the door leading down to the dungeons. Sadie catches me looking at it.

"Thinking about the Brass Key again?" she asks snarkily.

But instead of snapping back at her, I take it. After all, I'm the reason she and our friends are stuck here. And what Iggy just said—about me wanting her to look up to me and be proud of her big brother—has hit a nerve somewhere deep down. So all I say is, "Come on," as I lead the way upstairs, and I catch a flicker of surprise on Sadie's face.

The stone steps spiral upward, getting tighter as we

reach the top. I touch the stone walls and shiver at how icy cold they feel under my fingertips. *They're just padded gym mats*, I try to reassure myself, but it's all too scarily real. We could be walking through an *actual* medieval castle like the ones Mom and Dad dragged us through on vacation in the UK last summer.

At the top is a huge corridor that smells like fire-wood and incense. There are dim chandeliers and silent, creepy knights in full armor lined up along the walls. Behind each one is a large banner, all in different colors with different symbols. The knight to my immediate left stands well over six feet tall, and he's twice as wide as me in his dangerous-looking metal armor. His right hand, hidden inside a metal gauntlet, rests on the top of his sword. A large banner hangs behind him, depicting a vicious black bear with its fangs and claws bared.

"Were these here before?" Sadie asks Tom.

"Yeah, but something feels different," he says, his eyes darting around nervously.

"Whoa, they must be the Knights of the Round Table. Look," Jeremy says. He points at the end of the hall, where the doors to an enormous banquet hall have been left open. We can just see the edge of a gigantic circular table lined with curving benches.

"So which one is King Arthur?" Sadie asks nervously,

pressing closer to me as she looks at the scary knight in front of the bear banner.

"Why are you worrying about that?" Tom asks, his voice sharp with impatience. "It's the green flag we should worry about, and we need to get it *now* before anything else goes wrong."

I know it's probably nerves, but his tone annoys me. "Hey. Don't yell at my sister."

"I'm not yelling at her. I'm just trying to get her to focus."

"I *am* focused," Sadie tells him, clenching her teeth.

A low creak sounds out from somewhere in the hall.

"What was that?" Jeremy whispers.

"I don't know. But if it's the green team guarding their flag, we'd better get a move on," I say, lifting my phaser to my chest and aiming it into the darkness. "Tower's over there."

"Good, let's go." Tom sprints toward the stairs, not bothering to see if we're following.

"Hey! We stick together!" I call after him.

Creeeeeeeeaaaaaaaaak.

"That was louder this time," Sadie whispers, her phaser trembling in her hands.

"It's okay," I say, as she and Jeremy look up at me with worried faces. "You guys go ahead of me. Follow Tom. I'll cover you from behind."

They obey, and I swing around, walking backward with my phaser pointed out and my eyes on the supposedly empty hall behind us. And as I'm moving, I hear another ominous creak and see a movement out of the corner of my eye. The knight in front of the bear banner attracts my attention again. He is standing perfectly still, with his hands hanging at his sides.

"Wait a second," I mutter. I was *sure* his right hand had been on his sword earlier . . .

And just as the thought crosses my mind, the knight takes a step forward with a menacing *creeeeeeaaaaaaaakk* as his metal armor groans. He turns to face me, and even though there isn't any flicker of life inside the helmet, I can *feel* someone or something in there watching me.

"Um . . . guys?" I say, backing away slowly. "RUN, THE KNIGHTS ARE ALIVE!"

CHAPTER SEVENTEEN
SADIE

JEREMY AND I HAVE ALREADY REACHED THE TOWER stairs when Clip starts yelling. I whirl to see the Knights of the Round Table moving away from the walls, their movements stiff and unnatural and their armor creaking noisily as they surround my brother.

"Tom! Hold on!" Jeremy bellows up the stairs, but Tom is already scurrying back down, looking both frustrated and scared. And in a second, we see why: There are knights coming *down* at us from the tower, too. "We're being ambushed!"

"Clip!" I cry, as my brother disappears in the circle of terrifying metal men. My rational brain knows this is all fake and it's just a simulation. But I can't help shivering at the silent, menacing knights, their gauntlets moving toward the swords at their sides. There's no time to wonder what they *really* are or whether the swords will do damage. Clip got us into this mess, and he's arrogant and impulsive . . . but he's my brother. So I do the only thing I can think of.

I duck, and then dodge between the knights' legs.

"Sadie, no!" Jeremy shouts.

But I'm not the smallest player in the group for nothing. The knights are huge—probably well over six feet—so squeezing my way through the forest of metal knees and elbows is the work of only a few seconds for me. I don't have any plan other than reaching my brother.

Clip grabs my arm as soon as I get to him. "It's the banners, Sadie. Fire at the banners."

"What?" I sputter, as the knights press in closer around us.

He puts a hand on either side of my head and directs it toward the green bear banner. "See how each of them has a symbol? And then under the symbol . . ."

"A target," I breathe. I don't know why I didn't see it before. I try to angle my phaser, but the tall knights are blocking my view. "Jeremy! It's the banners! You have to aim—"

The *ping!* of a laser hits the bear banner before I even finish my sentence. The knight who had been stand-ing in front of it suddenly staggers back, like he's been

punched in the gut. In the gap in the circle, Clip and I
can see Jeremy's triumphant face.

"I got you!" he shouts, aiming at the banner again,
but this time he misses because the knight he's trying
to take out is *maaad*. He stumbles toward Jeremy with
one hand outstretched and the other on his sword, pulling it from the scabbard with the screeching sound of
metal.

"Oh, dang, the swords *are* real." I squeeze through a
gap in the circle and fire at the closest banner, a navy-
blue one with a phoenix symbol. Yet another knight

trips out of the circle and advances toward me as I keep hitting the target. "How many times do you have to hit it?"

"Three!" Tom yells, shooting at a red banner with a seal on it. "Jeremy and I will take this wall, and you guys work on the other one!"

Clip leaps over a couple of the fallen men to come help me. Slowly, one by one, we take out most of the knights. But there are six or seven who just won't go down.

"They're the ones from upstairs!" Tom calls. "Their banners must be up there."

"Come on, then! Let's go up!" Clip tears past the staggering knights and races up the tower steps, followed closely by the rest of us.

But the way is blocked.

At the top of the stairs is a knight with a billowing red velvet cloak. A five-pointed crown is painted onto the breastplate of his armor, and he carries a silver sword that is twice as long and wide as the other guys' weapons. He descends one step at a time, slowly and purposefully, the slits of his helmet focused directly on Clip.

"I think we found King Arthur," Jeremy mutters. He tries to dart around the newcomer to scurry up the steps, but the king seems to have guessed what he was doing. He stabs his sword into the wall of the tower, blocking the path, and Jeremy stops short with a squeak.

Without thinking, I fling myself around the king's other side. And being small pays off again, because I make it through and run up the steps.

"Find his banner, Sadie!" Clip yells.

At the top of the tower is a small round room, similar to the one Jeremy and I found in the Enchanted Forest. But the walls here are *covered* with banners, none of which have targets. All they display is the image of a cup or goblet. Some are encrusted with glittering gems, and others are made of plain metal. Some are huge, and some are as small as juice glasses. "Which one is it?" I mutter, my heart pounding. Somehow, this feels familiar. "Come on, Sadie, think."

The sound of loud clanking metal rings out from the stairwell, interrupting my frantic thoughts, and I whirl to see King Arthur climbing up to stop me from taking him out.

"Get him, Clip!" Jeremy shouts.

Clip throws himself over the top step, wrapping his arms around the king's legs. King Arthur tries to shake him off like a clingy puppy, but my brother holds on with all his strength.

As they struggle, Jeremy peers into the room. "You got this, Sadie! Think Indiana!"

"What?" I sputter. "What about Indiana? I've never even been there . . ."

"Indiana *Jones*, dummy!" Clip screams, still holding on to the king's legs.

I clap a hand over my forehead. Of course. This is why the scene feels familiar. Last month, Dad wanted to marathon these super-old movies about this dude named Indiana Jones, and he got Clip and Jeremy and me to watch with him. Indiana Jones is allegedly an archaeology professor, but instead of teaching in a classroom, he mostly gets to travel the world and look ruggedly handsome and steal ancient relics from jungles and stuff. Dad loves the franchise, but Mom always snorts and mutters something like, "That's nice, robbing cultures of their important artifacts," or "The way women are portrayed, I *swear* . . ."

Anyway, in the third movie, Indiana Jones ends up in this room full of goblets, and he has to find the Holy Grail among them. It's a trick challenge that he of course figures out. Instead of picking one of the pretty, shiny cups, he goes for this plain, busted-up old one.

As I'm remembering this, my eyes land on the banner with the ugliest, most boring goblet. I lift the edge and boom! There's a target underneath, and I fire at it. *Ping! Ping!*

"Yes! Good job! Keep going!" Clip shouts.

But somehow, King Arthur slips out of his grasp and thunders toward me in a crash of metal. I scurry out of the way and run face-first into the opposite wall. Clip and Jeremy lunge for the banner, but they fall flat a second later, their ankles grabbed by two of the remaining knights.

And then Tom somehow climbs over everybody and runs into the tower room. King Arthur sees him and flips out, but Tom manages to dodge him and reaches for me. I'm about to tell him not to worry about helping me and just hit the banner, when I see the look on his face: desperate, scared, and *determined*. He mutters something that might be an apology before he grabs my shoulder . . . and propels me toward King Arthur with an almighty push. My shoulder connects with a sheet of hard metal armor, and I wince as the king and I both crash to the floor.

"You did *not* just push Sadie, you little bug jerk!" Clip screams, still struggling with the knight who's holding on to his ankles.

Tom ignores him and lifts the Holy Grail banner, firing over and over at the target.

Everything goes still and silent. King Arthur stops struggling, and the metallic sound of the knights dies out. This one bull's-eye must have connected the king and all the remaining men.

Jeremy struggles to his feet and hurries over. "Sadie, are you okay?"

"Yeah, I . . ." I begin, but my voice is drowned out by Clip yelling at Tom. We turn to see my brother push Tom against the wall, hard.

"I saw that! You shoved my sister so you could have the glory!" Clip pushes him again, furious. "Don't *ever* touch her! You keep your stupid hands to yourself!"

"I *had* to do it, okay?" Tom argues. "She was in the way, and I needed someone to distract the king. And anyway, you would have done the same thing!"

My brother turns beet red. "That is *not* true!"

"Oh, come on, Clip. You would have pushed her to get the last shot if it had been you!"

"I'm nothing like you!" Clip shouts, and that launches an all-out fight. He and Tom collapse to the ground, wrestling and pounding each other in a tangle of furious fists.

"Guys, stop! Please!" Jeremy begs.

Footsteps pound up the stairs, and Caroline, Derek, and Iggy appear. At the sight of Tom and Clip brawling,

Iggy and Derek rush over to pull them apart. Neither are hurt, but the collar of Tom's T-shirt is askew and Clip's face is still bright red.

"What the heck is going on here?" Iggy demands.

Jeremy points at the king. "Tom pushed Sadie in front of *that* and Clip went nuts."

"Tom did *what*!" Derek exclaims, and the fury on his face makes my heart flutter a little.

"Let's deal with this later," Caroline says quickly. She grabs the green team's flag, which I hadn't noticed in all the commotion. "We took out the green team, but our purple 'teammates' have finally stopped making out and are on their way up here. We need to go."

"Make that door appear," Clip spits at Tom. "Get us back to the In-Between. Now!"

For a minute, I think Tom might refuse as he glares at my brother. But then he waves his hand and the door materializes, and everyone hurries back through it into the dark, sad little room. The computer screen is still up, and as I watch, the lights in the Haunted Castle sector snap on and the four teenagers head for the exit, looking a little confused but happy.

"All right. *Now* we can deal with this, you little twerp," my brother says, diving at Tom, but Derek and Iggy seize his arms just in time. "Let me go! Let me at him!"

"This isn't going to solve anything," Derek says,

straining from the effort of hanging on to Clip. "What are you gonna do? Kill him?"

"That's the idea," Clip snarls, still trying to lunge at Tom. "What were you thinking? I thought you were gonna try to be our teammate, with all your big talk, but I guess Sadie and Jeremy were right. You can't be trusted! I shouldn't have defended you!"

Tom flinches and presses himself against the wall.

"Calm down. Breathe," Iggy says, shaking Clip hard. After a moment, he and Derek let go, all three of them panting. "Tom, I think you owe Sadie an apology."

The boy's bug eyes turn to me. He's lost all of his bravado. "I'm sorry, Sadie," he says in a small voice, his knuckles white on his phaser. "I got caught up in the moment. I wanted to end the game and get us safely back here, and you were in the way, and . . ."

"*I* was going to end the game," I say, annoyed. "*You* got in *my* way."

"I'm sorry," Tom says again. "I didn't mean to hurt you. I was scared the arena might change again and throw us another curveball, and I panicked. Those knights have never been alive before." He hangs his head, his voice almost too quiet to hear. "I know it's not a good excuse, especially when you guys are stuck here helping me. I hope you'll forgive me."

I can hear in his voice that he means it, and some of

my anger fades. "If I aim at a target, I'm gonna hit it. So you don't need to push me aside. Got it?"

He nods, his eyes on his shoes. "Got it."

"I'm okay, Clip, honest. He didn't hurt me," I tell my brother, who puts his hand on my shoulder for a second before taking it away again. It's almost enough to stun me into silence, but I forge on, because I can see he's still *furious*. "Okay, so we only have the lab and the swamp."

"Two more battlegrounds. We got this, guys," Caroline says encouragingly, and the tension dissolves a bit. "As soon as a game ends in either one of those, we can jump in."

Jeremy checks the video feed. "Looks like both are still going strong."

Suddenly, the blank wall next to the computer screen starts flickering. Tom hurries over, shooting Clip a nervous glance, and calls up a keyboard that appears in midair. "It's just Aunt Lu wanting to check in," he explains, typing, and within seconds a woman's face shows up like a video chat, magnified to ten times its size and projected against the wall.

Even though Tom and Clip have told us all about Luellen Blackwood, the rest of us can't help jumping at the sight of her pale blue eyes roving over us in the In-Between.

"Tommy, I have great news! I'm . . . oh, wow!" she says, scanning the room. "Looks like a party. You hired yourself quite a crew."

Clip scowls, and Tom sees this and speaks up at once. "These are my new teammates. I had to trick them in here with me, and I feel awful, and I'm grateful for their help," he says hastily. "We just finished the Haunted Castle simulation."

"Good! Four down, two to go, huh?" Luellen smiles, which deepens the lines around her forehead and eyes. She looks almost as tired as Tom. "Thank you for helping my nephew, guys."

"It's not like we had a choice," Iggy mumbles. Luellen doesn't hear him say it, but Tom does and stares at the floor, his face downcast.

Luellen does a quick head count. "Seven of you. Good. The next two simulations are heavily team-based challenges. I was just at the front desk—I'm supposed to be on a bathroom break right now—but it looks like the lab game is winding down. You'll be headed there next."

"Yeah, look, the players are taking off their gear," Derek says, pointing at the screen.

Luellen nods. "That'll give you a ten-minute breather while the staff sweeps the arena."

"What were you saying about great news, Aunt Lu?" Tom interrupts.

The woman grins from ear to ear. "I am *this close* to getting the game to let you keep playing at night, even when the arena closes. I inputted those new commands this morning, and now I'm just waiting for the system to refresh and incorporate them into the code. Smooth sailing so far. If all goes well in the next half hour or so, you'll be able to continue tonight!"

Tom suddenly bends his knees and wiggles his whole upper body. His arms are flailing all around, and it takes everyone a second to realize he's dancing . . . really, *really* horribly, but still dancing. "Aunt Lu, I love you!" he shouts. "This is amazing! *You* are amazing!" He seems to realize we're all staring at him, so he stops the awful dancing. "Guys, don't you realize what this means? We'll have extra time to keep trying to get out of here! I've been going nuts every single night for three years, sitting in here and wishing I could keep going . . . and now we can! We could be out of here in, like, a couple of hours!"

Everybody cheers.

"We're getting out! We're getting out!" Jeremy and I say, hugging each other.

Even Clip looks thrilled by the news. "We're gonna crush this, team!"

"What can you tell us about the lab, Luellen?" Caroline asks eagerly. "Any tips?"

"And do you have any ideas on how the game might adapt?" Clip adds, scowling at Tom. "There have been a lot of . . . *unexpected* developments."

"Well, the Mad Scientist's Lab is the least popular simulation because there isn't a lot of running around or physical stuff," Luellen says thoughtfully. "Which I think is a shame, because it's fun. I designed it to be a puzzle battleground, with a series of escape rooms based on logic."

Jeremy and I look at each excitedly. "This is *definitely* Jer's area," I say, at the same time that my best friend says, "Sadie is *so* good at puzzles."

"Awesome," Clip says in his usual brisk tone, which means he's recovered from wanting to kill Tom. "All we need to do is escape the room, beat the swamp battleground, and then get out of the whole game. Every one of us."

An odd look crosses Luellen's face right then. I see her eyes cut to Tom, who stares back at her, but I seem to be the only one who notices because my friends are all busy talking about fun escape rooms they've done in the past. I'm about to call Tom out and ask what's going on when Iggy jabs a finger at the video feed for the Mad Scientist's Lab.

"Yo, get a load of those spring chickens!" he says, snickering.

A group of new players stands at the gate, ready to be let in, and none of them look a day *under* sixty-five. There are three women with curly white hair, their heads bent together like they're gossiping, and a man in an old-fashioned newsboy cap who is bent over a walker. Several other elderly people are using canes or wheelchairs. All of them look happy and excited to be there as they listen to the staff member, a high school kid with neon-blue hair, explain the rules.

"Maybe it's a bunch of friends from a nursing home or something," Jeremy suggests.

Derek snorts. "Geriatric laser tag. Now *this* I gotta see."

Caroline punches his arm. "Shut up, Derek! Old people can play, too. There aren't any *maximum* age restrictions in the arena."

"And Luellen said there isn't a lot of physical stuff involved here," I point out.

"There's also a bingo room," Luellen says. "I bet that's where these folks are headed."

"Bingo?" Clip repeats incredulously.

"It's still themed," the game designer says, her voice almost defensive. "Each person gets a grid of twenty-five test tubes, all containing different potion ingredients. When an ingredient is called out, anyone who has that tube dumps it into a beaker. Whoever gets a bingo and creates a special potion wins the game, and the simulation ends."

"You know, I never got why Grandma and Grandpa liked bingo so much," I say to Clip thoughtfully. "But that sounds kind of fun."

Tom shakes his head. "But we can't go in there, remember? The players can't know that we're in the game, so we'll have to pick another room."

"You'll need to wait until they're settled in the bingo room," Luellen agrees. "I designed the Mad Scientist's Lab simulation to look like a spooky old mansion. There's a hall of doors, and behind each of the doors is a separate challenge. Your team could wait in the parlor, Tom."

I see Clip bristle at her suggestion that the group is *Tom's* team.

"Okay, so we just have to pick another door. Which is the easiest?" Iggy asks.

"We don't need easy, Ig," Caroline says, snorting. "We have Sadie and Jer, remember?"

"Yeah, we got our big brains with us," Clip says, and Jeremy and I grin at each other. Our whole team believes in us, *including* my brother. "We don't need easy; we need fun and exciting. So which is the best challenge to pick?"

"Fun and exciting. Well, the door at the end of the hall

is the *true* basement laboratory," Luellen says. "There are riddles and a potion challenge."

We all look at each other, feeling excited despite how serious the situation is.

Luellen checks a monitor beside her. "Okay, it looks like the old folks are in. And I need to get back to the front desk and keep an eye on the new code override," she says. "Remember to wait a bit in the parlor before you go down the hall, just to make sure they're all inside the bingo room and won't see you. And then you'll only have about fifteen minutes left to win."

"Got it, Aunt Lu," Tom says, and her face disappears. "Are you guys ready to go in?"

Clip shrugs. "Call up the door."

Tom obeys, and then we're all plunging back through the glowing door into the arena.

CHAPTER EIGHTEEN
CLIP

LUELLEN SAID SHE DESIGNED THIS BATTLEGROUND to look like a spooky old mansion, and boy, did she succeed, because I feel like we've entered the set of a horror movie.

We're standing in what must be the parlor, this long, low chamber that has beat-up wood floors. Even the wallpaper, which is dark blue with weird black zigzag patterns, looks haunted. The place is lit only with flickering candles, and outside the windows, it's night and rain is splattering against the glass. Instead of the hip-hop and dance music that's played in all the other battlegrounds, there's some kind of eerie, slow opera piping through the speakers.

"This place gives me the creeps," I hear Sadie whisper to Jeremy.

"Yo, check out this stuff on the wall," Derek says, staring up at a bunch of tools nailed to the wallpaper. There are hammers of all sizes, rusty pliers, long implements with little mirrors at the end, syringes, and other sharp, shiny items that look like they're meant for surgery.

Caroline gags. "Gross! That syringe has something brownish on the needle."

"It's probably blood from someone's tetanus shot." Derek reaches over and gives her a sharp, playful pinch on the arm, and she yells and whacks her brother upside the head.

Meanwhile, Iggy's on the opposite side of the room, busy walking back and forth in front of some paintings. "Hey, come look at these old people. Their eyes follow you no matter where you go," he tells Sadie and Jeremy, who imitate him and pace in front of them. "Why, yes, I was born here even if I'm brown, Lord Crumpetbottom!"

"No, I'm not from the Orient, Lady Dustfeather! Stop staring at me!" Sadie tells the portrait of a snooty-looking woman, and Jeremy doubles over, laughing at their comments.

I'm grinning at everyone's shenanigans when Tom comes up beside me.

"Hey, Clip? I'm sorry again about pushing Sadie," he

says. He looks nervous, and I can't say I blame him . . . I *did* almost try to kill him back at the Haunted Castle. "This is just the best chance I've had of getting out in years, and I got carried away. I know it's not a good excuse."

"It's cool, man," I say. "I mean, it's *not* cool. But apology accepted. You're under stress."

He sighs. "It's this thing with my mom and aunt, too. They're mad at each other and keep venting to me. Mom's always talking trash about Aunt Lu, and Aunt Lu wants me to keep her a secret. It's exhausting. I just wanna be a kid and, like, play laser tag and soccer and stuff."

"It sucks when grown-ups pull us into their mess," I agree, remembering how sad and kind Mardella had seemed when we had met her that first night. But I guess a person can show one side to strangers and a whole other side to their family. I think of how I am when I'm around my family and how I am when I'm with my friends, and squirm a bit. Quickly, I change the subject. "You mentioned soccer? Do you play?"

"Yeah. I was a center midfielder in my summer league."

"Wait, that's the position *I* play!"

"Really?" Tom asks, brightening. "I miss soccer. That feeling you get when the whistle blows and the ball starts moving, and it's like everyone's part of this machine."

"And if you all do your part, you inch closer and closer to that goal," I add.

"There's nothing like it. Anyway, I feel bad about what I did, and I hope we can be a team again." He holds out his hand and I shake it, feeling a lot friendlier toward him. I mean, who knows what being stuck in the game for years would do to *me*?

Iggy, Sadie, and Jeremy have found a door tucked against the side of a china cabinet and are trying to budge it open. "There's no knob, but press all along the edges," Jeremy suggests. "There might be some kind of hidden spring. I learned that from the Hardy Boys."

"Who are the Hardy Boys?" Iggy asks, applying pressure all over the door.

"Characters from this super-old book series. My dad had a few copies lying around the house and I read them out of curiosity," Jeremy explains, crouching down to feel along the bottom edge of the door. "They're, like, ancient. Probably published in 1990 or something."

"Aha!" Sadie suddenly cries, and the door pops out slightly from the wall.

"Hold up, hold up, guys," Tom says, hurrying over. "That might be an emergency exit."

"An emergency exit?" Jeremy repeats, his eyes gleaming. "Like, out of the arena? So if we went through it, we could potentially get out of the game?"

Everyone starts talking all at once, excited, but I hang back. I've played a lot of games in my time, and I've learned never to trust shortcuts.

"I keep telling you guys. There's no way out of the game except to play it through and win," Tom says patiently. "I've been stuck here for three years. You really think I haven't gone through every single option, including emergency exits? Here. Poke your head around the door and look, but keep your feet inside. If you leave the simulation, this game will be over for us."

"It'll be like we lost?" Iggy asks.

Tom nods, and one by one, we peek carefully out of the emergency exit. When it's my turn, I see a familiar dark space with a stack of padded mats, a low shelf full of phasers, and a computer screen that shows the video feed from all six sectors of the arena.

"It's the In-Between Room," Jeremy says, confused. "Everything leads back there?"

"Everything leads back there. But only the glowing door I pull up counts," Tom says, firmly shutting the door. "If you try to use the emergency exits, it doesn't work."

"Wow. We really *are* stuck," Sadie says in a small voice, coming to stand close to me.

I pat her shoulder. "Like Tom said, we just have to play our way through. Speaking of which, maybe it's time to get this show on the road? Those old people must be gone by now."

Tom nods in agreement. "Follow me."

We trail after him down a long hallway that's lit only by flashes of lightning from the simulated storm outside. There are six closed doors, and as we pass one, we hear people chatting and laughing. The bingo tournament's in full swing. Tom takes us to the last door, and we all file into a room that's a little smaller than the parlor. The ceiling, floor, and walls are all made of stone, and the space is laid out kind of like the chemistry lab at school, with two long counters separated by aisles. Beakers, flasks, and test tubes line the counters, and all along the walls of the room is a circular conveyor belt, like the kind at the airport where you collect your suitcases.

As we watch, the conveyor belt switches on, and a bunch of jars and bowls and different kinds of containers start coming out of an opening on the opposite wall. Each of them has a blank white label with only a big bull's-eye target on it.

"They're potion ingredients," Sadie says eagerly. "Looks like we have to find the right ones and aim our lasers at them."

"Um, okay. *That's* new," Tom mutters, and everyone turns to see what he's looking at.

In the far corner of the room is a big gold hourglass with grains of sand already slipping through it. It's attached to a huge metal cage that has a padlock on the door, and inside the cage paces a very angry-looking, very *realistic* gray timber wolf, its dark red eyes fixed hungrily on us. It sees us staring and lets out this deep, terrifying growl.

"What do you mean, new? There's never been a wolf before?" Derek asks nervously.

Tom shakes his head, his face pale. "This is another adaptation of the game."

"I don't care if it's not real. It is *inhumane* to keep a wild animal locked up like this." Annoyed, Caroline walks over and checks the padlock. When she lifts it slightly, we see that it's connected to the hourglass. "So what's the objective of the game? Free the wolf?"

"I don't think it's about freeing the wolf," Jeremy says slowly, and everyone looks at him. "I think it's about *not letting time run out*. Because when all the sand goes through that hourglass, the cage door is going to open, and then . . ."

"We're all dead meat," Iggy says.

"Not dead. This isn't real," Derek says, sounding like he's trying to convince himself.

"Come on, we got this," Jeremy says confidently, looking at Sadie. "So that's the object. We have to solve riddles or whatever before the hourglass runs out. Where are the riddles?"

Sadie points at the counter. "Here we go! Eight pieces of paper, each with a riddle on it."

Jeremy is about to grab the first piece of paper, but then he stops and looks at me. "Um, do you . . . do you mind if Sadie and I take the lead on this one?"

"Yeah, go for it. You guys are good at this stuff. The rest of us will hang tight and do whatever you need to help." I catch sight of my sister staring at me, her mouth hanging open in shock. "What, Sadie?" I ask, offended. "If I'm going to be captain of the soccer team one day, I need to be able to *delegate* tasks to people who are best at them, right?"

Iggy high-fives me. "Hey, man, that was a good word!"

I smirk at my sister. "I've been saying it all along: Sadie's not the only smart Chu."

"Keep your mouth closed, so my good opinion of you lasts longer," Sadie says in a sassy voice, as she and Jeremy hold up the first riddle and we all crowd around them.

It's handwritten on a piece of crinkly, tan paper that looks like parchment, and I gotta hand it to Mardella . . . I mean, Luellen. There's nothing more old-timey than writing with a pen.

Jeremy clears his throat and reads the poem aloud:

This challenge will be your race against time.
Let's hope that your brains are all at their prime.
A furious wolf is pacing the cage.
You must solve seven riddles, page by page,
And the answers will point you, straight and true,
To a recipe you will need to brew.
Add to the cauldron before time is up
And you'll make that beast no more than a pup.

Iggy scratches his head. "What does *that* mean? 'Make that beast no more than a pup'?"

"And what recipe are they talking about?" Derek adds, riffling through the other papers.

"Stop, they might be in a certain order!" Jeremy scolds him. He and Sadie exchange looks that say, *These guys are hopeless.* "It sounds like each of these riddles will give us a potion ingredient that we need to find on that conveyor belt, and then we put it into that cauldron." He points to a big black pot on one counter. "Once we mix them up, we feed the potion to the wolf."

"And turn it into a puppy?" Caroline asks, squinting at the poem.

"I don't know if it will *literally* turn into a puppy," Sadie says, "but the potion's going to make the wolf harmless. Either way, when time runs out, that cage door is gonna pop open."

Everyone looks around at each other for a moment.

I shrug. "I guess let's make sure the wolf is cute and cuddly when that happens."

CHAPTER NINETEEN
CLIP

EVERYONE PRESSES IN CLOSE AROUND SADIE AND
Jeremy, but I decide to stand on the outside and await
further instruction. My sister complains about how big-
headed I am, but I *know* my weaknesses, and one is riddles. Can't wrap my head around them. Obviously, I'm
smart. I'm just not patient enough to figure out weird
little poems, like Sadie and Jeremy are. Their faces
remind me of how I feel on the soccer field: confident,
excited, and ready to crush the opponent.

I stare at the potion ingredients moving slowly past
on the conveyor belt and poke Derek in the back. "Hey,
D, doesn't this remind you of . . ."

"The Sushi Raceway?" Derek asks, and we both burst
into laughter. There's a reason Derek has been my best
friend since *forever*, and it's because we pretty much

share the same brain. "That restaurant was *so* good. It was fun picking whatever little plates of sushi you wanted off the conveyor belt. I'm still bummed that place closed."

My stomach rumbles at the memory of the delicious bites of sushi. "Remember those crunchy crab rolls? And how stressed you got about whether to take this plate or that plate before it disappeared and someone else nabbed it?"

Derek snickers, but we both fall silent when Sadie turns around and glares at us. "Do you two mind?" she asks, then clears her throat and reads the first riddle out loud.

I am warm and full of zest.
This will be a fragrant quest.
Rubbery skin but sweet within,
With juice that drips right down your chin.

Derek and I look at each other blankly. "Sounds like some kind of . . . fruit?" I venture.

"Orange peel," Sadie says with absolute certainty. "Do you guys mind looking in those jars and containers for some? Jeremy and I can get started on the next riddle."

"That wasn't so bad," Jeremy says brightly.

I shrug and start scanning the conveyor belt with Derek and Caroline, opening pots and peering into jars. Might as well make ourselves useful, right? Who says I'm not the *best* team player? As we search the various items, we hear Jeremy reading the second riddle out loud.

My matrix is a honeycomb.
The human body is my home.
I may be strong, but still can break.
Plenty of calcium you must take.

"The human body . . ." Derek mutters as he moves jars around, still searching for the orange peel. He glances at Caroline. "Any ideas?"

"Don't look at me. I flunked science." She picks up a small bowl with a lid and peers inside it. "*Aha!* Here are the orange peels! I'll take care of 'em." She aims her phaser at the bull's-eye target on the bowl, then dumps the contents into the cauldron.

We all cheer, and then go back to scratching our heads over the riddle.

"Honeycomb," Tom says thoughtfully. "Is the ingredient honey?"

"Honey isn't strong or breakable," Sadie tells him, with a withering look. I grin, wishing I could bottle that look and unleash it whenever I want. "And the poem says honeycomb *matrix.*"

Tom raises his eyebrows. "Ooooookay . . . so what does that mean?"

"Human bones have a honeycomb matrix. It's their structure. We just learned that in science," Jeremy says. "So I think we're looking for a skeleton, or maybe some small bones."

"Like these?" Iggy, who's standing on the far end of the conveyor belt, asks. He's holding a jar and what looks like a bouquet of finger bones. "Man, I hope these are plastic."

"Throw 'em in the cauldron!" Sadie says happily. He fires at the jar's bull's-eye, then adds the bones to the cauldron as she reads the third riddle.

I am a small eight-pointed star.
My flavor's hailed both near and far.
From five spice to boiling soups,
When it comes to taste, there are no dupes.

My sister reads the poem again, mouthing the words. And then, with everyone watching, she bursts into a laugh that I can only describe as *villainous.* She even tips her chin to the ceiling like she's taken over the world or something. "Good thing there's a Vietnamese kid here.

Even *you* would know this, Clip. What's the most important ingredient of Grandma's pho?"

I rack my brain. "That weird little star thing she flavors the broth with."

"Ding ding ding! We're looking for star anise!" Sadie says triumphantly. She bends down and looks at the wolf in the cage. "You're going to be a nice puppy in no time."

The wolf lifts its lip in answer, revealing a row of razor-sharp, blindingly white teeth.

"Let's not tease the doggie, sis," I say, locating the star anise on the conveyor belt behind a jar of cinnamon sticks. They're about the size of a quarter and smell really

strong. I fire at the bull's-eye, glad to be doing something to contribute, and dump the stars into the cauldron.

Iggy peers at the hourglass. "How much time do you think we have left?"

"Maybe six or seven minutes. We gotta hurry, though," Tom says, bouncing up and down on his toes. "Those old people will probably be finishing their bingo tournament soon."

"Okay, let's speed this up. Here's the fourth riddle," Jeremy says, reading it aloud.

I'm born from the seeds of a tree.
The tropics is where you'll find me.
When raw, I have a bitter taste.
But you'll eat milk or white in haste!

"Is it coffee?" Iggy asks hopefully. His mom is a manager at the local coffee factory. "Coffee beans are seeds, I guess. And they're from the tropics, and coffee tastes bitter."

"But what about the milk or white part?" I ask. "You add milk to coffee, but *white*?"

"They sound like kinds of chocolate." Caroline looks stunned at herself as Sadie and Jeremy both clap and grin at her. "The answer's chocolate!"

The twins hunt for the candy as Sadie picks up the

next riddle. Only two to go after this, and even though we're doing well, I can't help looking at the hourglass again. The wolf seems to be more restless by the minute. It catches my eye and bares its teeth again. *It's just a block of code, not a real wolf,* I tell myself, trying to pay attention as my sister reads the next poem.

We're fit for the Underworld's queen
With our tart and rosy pink sheen.
Six seeds for six months of sunshine.
Birds sing and fruits bloom on the vine.

"The Underworld? Like, in Greek myth? I didn't know that place had a queen," Iggy says, looking confused. "In that old Disney movie, the blue-fire-hair guy wasn't married."

Tom stares blankly at him. "What are you even *talking* about?"

"You know. Hades, the god of the Underworld. Right? Am I on the right track?" Iggy snaps his fingers. "*Hercules.* That's the name of the movie."

Sadie, the reigning expert of movies-that-came-out-way-before-we-were-even-born, nods excitedly. "You're on the right track. Hades was married to Persephone. She was some kind of goddess, I think. They left her out of the

Disney movie, but he basically stole her from her mom and brought her to the Underworld to be his queen."

"Why would anyone want to *steal* another person?" Iggy asks, puzzled. "Wouldn't it be better to ask first? Or find someone who actually wants to marry you?"

Caroline points at him in approval. "It's called consent, my dude."

Sadie claps her hands. "I remember now! Persephone won't eat because she's sad about, like, getting kidnapped. So Hades brings her a pomegranate, her favorite. And she eats six seeds, so they decide that six months out of the year she'll stay with him . . . That's fall and winter . . ."

"And the other six months, she'll go back to the world above with her mom, for spring and summer," Jeremy adds, nodding. "Nice, Sadie! We're looking for pomegranate seeds, guys!"

"On it." Iggy and Tom jump into action and start searching the conveyor belt.

"Okay, riddle number six," Jeremy says, picking up the second-to-last poem. Behind him, the wolf growls, attracting our nervous attention.

I'm a sweet and sticky delight.
Infection? I'll put up a fight.

Put me in your food or your tea,
And don't forget to thank the bees.

"Oh, that's an easy one." Derek pulls a jar of honey off the conveyor belt, looking to Sadie and Jeremy for confirmation. "But *does* it fight infection?"

"Yep. Honey has antibacterial effects," my sister says, picking up the final riddle.

I peek at the wolf, which slowly scrapes a front paw across the bars, its eyes glinting with what looks uncomfortably like hunger. To my horror, the top half of the hourglass is almost empty. "Hey, guys, I don't want to sound pushy or anything, but the sand is getting reeeeeeeaaally low," I say. "Maybe speed this up?"

"Everything's in the cauldron now," Derek calls, from where he and Iggy have finished adding the pomegranate seeds and honey. "We'll be ready to find whatever's next."

"Okay. Here we go," Sadie says, reading the last poem out loud.

We are fragile and white as snow,
Fade in bouquets, but florists know
Our childish scent lends a special air
And gives any vase quite a flair.

Everyone looks at each other, bewildered. Even Jeremy and Sadie look stumped.

"Bouquets and florists . . . so we're looking for a flower, right?" Caroline asks, as she, Derek, and Iggy leap into action, searching the conveyor belt. "We've been through all the containers six times by now and I don't remember seeing any flowers."

"*Our childish scent?* What do they smell like? Froot Loops?" I ask incredulously.

"We know they're white," Sadie mutters, as she and Jeremy join in the search. "White flowers . . . It said 'fade in bouquets,' so they can't be big . . ."

I glance at Tom and see that he's on the verge of panicking again. He knocks over a few jars as he searches desperately, his face almost angry. "You okay, dude?" I ask him.

But he's so freaked out, he doesn't hear me. "Stay calm," he mutters to himself. "We'll win, and I'll be the first one out the door. I'm not the one who has to stay behind this time."

"First one out the door, huh?" I repeat, and he looks up in shock, only just realizing that I've heard him. From where she's standing, Sadie looks up, listening as she glances between Tom and me. "You think we're going to leave you in the game like those other kids did?"

"I . . ."

"What kind of people do you think we are?" I ask, as everyone else is frantically looking for the flowers. "I thought we were a team. Why don't you trust us?"

Before Tom can say anything, Iggy starts yelling, "Whoa, whoa, whoa!" He snatches up a vase of flowers that was hidden behind some tall canisters on the conveyor belt. It's got red and yellow roses, surrounded by green ferns and some kind of frilly white blossoms.

"Baby's breath! It's baby's breath!" Sadie shrieks, pointing at the crumbly white flowers.

The last grains of sand are running through the hourglass . . . slipping . . . slipping . . .

Derek points frantically at the cauldron. "Put them in! Put them in!"

Iggy fires his phaser at the bull's-eye on the vase, rips the stems out, and tosses them into the cauldron. At that exact moment, both the conveyor belt and the hourglass stop. The cage opens, the metal hinges creaking loudly, and the wolf races out. Together, Iggy and Derek throw the cauldron in front of it, and it lowers its head and starts to eat. The red gleam of its eyes fades, and when it's done with the weird meal, it sits back on its haunches and looks at all of us, furry head tipped to one side. It's . . . cute.

"Good wolfie," Caroline croons, kneeling beside it. It

opens its mouth, and a long pink tongue hangs out as it pants, reminding me of Tofu. "Who's a good wolf?"

"We did it, team. Good work," I say, exchanging high fives with everyone . . . except Tom, who hangs back, still looking a little awkward.

"We have to get back to the In-Between. Quick!" he says, and the glowing door—now familiar to everyone in the room—materializes in a corner of the lab.

One by one, we charge back inside, fresh from our victory.

CHAPTER TWENTY
SADIE

THE MINUTE THE DOOR CLOSES BEHIND US, MY brother turns to Tom. "So, you feel like explaining what I just heard? About how you're planning to jump out the door first when we beat the game, like we're all gonna abandon you or something?" Clip demands.

All eyes turn to Tom, who looks miserable. "Listen, I've been in here for three years. Can you *blame* me for wanting to make sure I get out?" He holds up his hands. "I know you guys aren't like those other kids. But I just can't take that chance again."

Jeremy, Iggy, and I look at each other and shrug. His explanation sounds reasonable enough, but Clip is frowning and still looking suspicious.

"It's one thing to be annoyed about getting trapped," Derek says. "But it's another thing to just leave a person behind. You didn't deserve that, man. Not then or now."

"Thanks." Tom is quiet for a moment, fidgeting with the hem of his shirt as he looks around at all of us. "Hey, guys? I have to . . . There's something I want to . . ."

The blank wall next to the computer screen starts flashing again, interrupting him.

"Sorry, hang on. That's Aunt Lu." He breaks off his sentence and hurries over to pull up the keyboard. Within seconds, Luellen Blackwood's face appears on the wall again.

"You're back! I'm assuming it went well?" she asks eagerly.

"Really well. Everyone was great, especially Sadie and Jeremy, who solved the riddles," Tom says, pointing us out. And even though I *still* don't trust him, I have to admit I like him better for giving credit where credit's due. "We beat the game just in the nick of time."

"Well done," Luellen says approvingly. "You're all very close to the end now. I have to say, Tommy, I'm glad you put together such a great team and got them all so far."

"Hang on a second, *we* all got ourselves this far," I say, annoyed. "It's not just thanks to Tom, you know. Everyone contributed their skills."

"He might have the experience, being stuck in the game all these years," Clip adds, looking just as irritated, "but he definitely needed a team leader like me."

I scowl at my brother. "You mean, he needed a *team*. Victory doesn't come down to just one person. You wouldn't have even gotten past the Deadly Cliffs if not for me. Remember?" I let out a strangled growl of frustration when he only responds with a confused look. "Did you forget already? I stopped the egg from rolling off the mountainside when *you* overshot it!"

"Sadie's right," Jeremy says at once. "And everyone took down the roc together, and in the Haunted Castle, we had to team up to get those zombie knights."

"Yeah! So why are you taking all the credit?" I demand, looking at Clip.

"I'm not," my brother says, baffled. "I just said that Tom needed—"

"A team leader like you. That's what you said, word for word." Everyone's heads are moving between us like they're at a tennis match, but I don't care. Clip isn't going to get the last word this time. "You always have to be the center of attention. And what would you have done if you hadn't had me and Jeremy to solve the riddles, huh?"

"We would have figured them out. *Now* who's giving themselves too much credit?"

I feel my chest puff up with hot air. I'm about to unleash another bout of fury on him when Luellen laughs. "You two are *definitely* siblings," she says. "This is exactly how Mardella and I used to fight. Blaming each other and accomplishing nothing, and now her son's stuck in the game. Don't you think it's time to put aside these silly arguments and get out, children?"

I glare at Clip and he rolls his eyes, but we fall silent.

"Come on, guys, we're almost done," says Derek, the peacemaker. "I'm sure we can leave tonight. We just have to get through the Swamp of Despair."

"Aunt Lu, how did that code override work out?" Tom asks urgently, checking the video feed of the arena. "Looks like the whole place is about to close."

We look at the screen, which shows people exiting and the lights in each sector shutting down. Staff members move through the space, sweeping and mopping and replacing fallen mats. I check my watch, horrified, and realize it's now 9:00 p.m.

"What are we gonna do?" Caroline asks Derek, panicking. "This place doesn't open again until eleven a.m., and Dad will freak out if we aren't home by then."

"Hold on. The system incorporated my override

perfectly, just as I expected, and I'll be able to manipulate the code so you can enter the final game without
any real players," Luellen says confidently, and Caroline
lets out a huge sigh of relief. "We just have to wait for the
staff to close up and leave. Tom, in the meantime, I'm
going to need you to enter a few commands on your side.
Can you hit 'Control' on your keyboard, and then . . ."

As Tom focuses on the keys, following her instructions, Clip waves us all over.

"What is it?" I ask, once everyone has huddled up.

"It's something Tom said," he says in a low voice.
"Back in the Mad Scientist's Lab. He said he wanted to
be the first one out the door, no matter what."

"He explained that," I tell him.

"I know. But I also heard him say he doesn't want to
be the one who has to stay behind this time." Clip frowns.
"The one who *has* to stay behind. Isn't that a weird way
to put it?"

Jeremy furrows his brow. "It almost sounds like . . ."

"Like someone has to be left behind in the game?" I
say softly.

There's a silence.

Clip chews on his bottom lip. "Maybe . . . maybe the
game has gotten used to having someone in here. To
keep it stable. Maybe there always has to be *one* person

inside. And this kid is desperate," he adds. "Like, *desperate*. I was ready to kill him when he shoved Sadie, and then in the lab, he got all hot and bothered when he thought we were gonna lose."

Jeremy stares at him, wide-eyed. "So if someone *has* to be left behind in the game . . ."

"Tom's gonna make sure it won't be him this time," Iggy finishes.

We all look at each other.

Clip peers over his shoulder to where Tom is still clacking away at the green keyboard. "Listen, guys, I was starting to . . . well, not exactly *like* the kid, but respect him, at least. He's a lot like me, smart and competitive and resourceful," he says, ignoring me when I give a loud snort. "But if all this is true, we can't trust him. Don't let on that we know about this, and when we beat this swamp level, let's keep him away from the glowing door. Okay?"

"You're worried he's going to run right through?" Caroline whispers.

"So he won't be the one who stays, and one of us might," Iggy says darkly. "Wow."

"*If* someone has to be left behind," Jeremy points out. "We're just guessing here. But it's better to be safe than sorry. And now that we suspect this, we can prepare."

"Hey. Are you guys having a team meeting without me?" Tom asks, right behind Clip. We all give a guilty jump, and I can tell everyone else is wondering how much he heard, too.

"Just giving the crew a pep talk before we dive in," Clip says casually. "Ready to go?"

Tom points to the video feed of the arena, which is now completely empty. Only one sector is brightly lit: the Swamp of Despair. "Aunt Lu saw all the staff members get in their cars and leave, so the coast is clear. I hope that pep talk worked, because we're gonna need it."

Iggy studies his grim expression. "You think the game's going to change again?"

The boy nods, his wide bug eyes serious. "Everything that's been new so far has been really big. Like, the roc? The hedge maze and zombie knights? And the wolf in the cage? This is already the toughest battleground, and we're going to need to stay alert in there."

"It's our last chance at freedom," Caroline says, and I can almost hear Jeremy next to me thinking the same thing: *Maybe not for one of us.* "Might as well give it a shot."

"And we're a team." Clip looks right at Tom, his face stern and serious, and I can see in that moment exactly why he's been tapped for captainship of the soccer team. "Right?"

Tom swallows hard but doesn't look away from my brother when he answers, "Right."

Derek shrugs. "Okay. Well, let's call up that door and get in there."

And then we're plunging back into the arena one last time . . . I hope.

CHAPTER TWENTY-ONE
SADIE

I SEE RIGHT AWAY WHY THIS BATTLEGROUND IS called the Swamp of Despair. We've entered a dense, vast woodland that's way darker and hotter than the Enchanted Forest. Everywhere we look, there are twisted gray tree trunks and slimy vines dangling down. There's a creepy feel to the place, what with the unnatural quiet and the heavy silver mist that hangs low over it. The air has a moldy, earthy smell, with the underlying scent of a dumpster in midsummer.

Caroline pinches the end of her nose. "Whew, that's a nice bouquet. Smells kind of like that time Derek left a pizza slice under the couch for a week."

"I was on the floor playing video games and I forgot, okay?" her twin protests.

Clip narrows his eyes at Tom. "So what's the objective here?"

"Every time I've played it, the goal has been to cross that giant swamp." Tom points through the thicket of trees. We can make out the edge of a cloudy body of water that's a deep radioactive-green color. "It's harder than it sounds because you have to jump across logs and boulders and stuff, like an obstacle course. It'll take a lot of balance."

"That sounds fine," Clip says, exchanging eager glances with Derek and Caroline.

But Jeremy and I look at each other, worried. "Balance? This sounds pretty physical," he says, right as I'm saying, "Is there an alternate route Jer and I can take?"

"No. The only way to the end is across," Tom says. "And at the end, we have to complete some kind of puzzle. Aunt Lu designed it to change with every game, but usually it involves putting something together. The banshee will tell us."

Derek blinks. "Banshee? Isn't that, like, some kind of ghost?"

"A banshee is typically a woman," Jeremy explains. "According to folklore, she screams outside people's windows at night when they're about to die, and—"

Right on cue, a bloodcurdling shriek echoes through the woodland. Iggy yells in surprise, and Caroline steps backward onto Clip's foot in her shock. The scream raises every hair on the back of my neck, and I press close to Jeremy despite the heat. Even Tom, who expected it, looks unnerved. But it lasts for only a few seconds, and then the woodland is quiet again.

"Sounds a little like Clip playing *War of Gods and Men*," I say weakly.

"Ha, ha, very funny," my brother says, his face pale.

"The shore is where the banshee gives us instructions. Come on," Tom says, leading us.

We move through the thick, pungent underbrush, twigs crackling and ferns rustling. I jostle a wet tree branch, and some of the dew flicks off onto my hand. This is definitely the most realistic simulation so far, and I don't like it. Jeremy sticks by my side, looking anxious.

Soon, the trees clear out to reveal a shallow bank of mossy dirt, which darkens from a moldy mushroom color to outright black where it meets the dank water. The swamp stretches out in front of us like a puddle of goo. It's wider than I thought, maybe fifty feet across, and is full of *stuff*. Ragged plants, rotting vines, and other vegetation cover the surface, and there are rocks and thick logs laid lengthwise, just wide enough for someone to walk across.

A tall, slender figure in black appears. It's covered from head to toe in frayed, ripped-off cloth, the torn edges swaying as it moves. There is no way to tell what it looks like because its whole head is hidden. As it speaks, the cloth over its mouth moves gently and eerily.

"Welcome to the Swamp of Despair," it says in a low, scratchy voice, like it's suffering from a terrible chest cold. I notice that the fluttering edges of the cloth are covered with a thick, sticky reddish liquid that looks a *whole* lot like blood, and I can see from my friends' gaping faces that they've seen it, too. "You are brave . . . very brave indeed to come here. Or is it stupid?" A low, evil laugh rattles from the banshee's hidden mouth.

"It's just a game," I hear Jeremy whisper to himself. "Just a game, just a game."

Tom opens his mouth to reply to the banshee, but Clip dives right in and takes charge before he can say anything. "Thanks for the welcome," my brother says in a brisk voice. "I hear the challenge is to cross the swamp to the other side?"

"The challenge is to cross the swamp to the other side," the banshee says in a robotic way, pointing a dramatic black-gloved finger toward the far end of the water. It's almost like it didn't hear Clip's question, which weirdly makes me feel a little better.

"See? It's just an NPC," I say reassuringly to Jeremy. "It can't understand us."

"It may sound simple, but it will be difficult to cross," the banshee goes on. "You will face many obstacles, some of which you can see before you and some you won't until too late." Again, it utters that creepy laugh. "If you fall into the water, you *must* return here and start all over again. Otherwise, the team's victory will not count at the end."

"Dang, really?" Iggy mutters.

"Everyone must set foot on that far island, no matter how briefly. Once there, you must put together the Statue of the Silver Monkey, an ancient relic that has been lost to the sands of time. Until now." The banshee pauses, allowing this to sink in. "Successfully completing this task will activate and lower a series of wooden bridges, allowing all of you to retrace your steps across the swamp and bring me that statue. You have thirty minutes. Begin."

Now done with its spiel, the banshee begins to glide backward swiftly and silently, like it's on wheels on a track. It's the freakiest image: the slender body moving without walking, gloved hands outstretched, and the ragged black cloth fluttering with the movement.

For a second, we all just stare across the swamp.

"The statue's our puzzle this time around, I guess," Tom says. He points to the logs. "Just be careful about going across those, because sometimes they move under you and make you lose your balance. Go slowly, and try not to fall in the water if you can avoid it."

Jeremy and I look nervously at each other. Neither of us wants to be the last person to get on that island and back, but one of us probably will be.

"What sort of obstacles did you have last time?" Iggy asks, studying the water.

"One time, there were only logs. No boulders. Another time, there was a swinging rope bridge that led all the way across. It sounds easy," Tom adds, "but it kept shaking hard with every move I made, and some of the planks were rotten and broke under my feet. Trust me, it's a good thing that bridge isn't here this time around. Those wooden ones look a lot better."

We follow his gaze and see a series of five or six sturdy wooden bridges, scattered down the middle of the swamp. All of them are pointed straight in the air, but we can see cogs and cables that will lower them so that they all connect.

"I wish they were down right now," Jeremy says anxiously.

"That would defeat the purpose," Clip tells him in a businesslike tone. "Getting across wouldn't be fun if it wasn't hard. And once we complete that puzzle, they *will* come down."

"I guess we should start," I say, my throat dry.

Tom looks at my brother. "Clip, do you want to take the lead? Or do you want me to go first, since I've already been here? I don't mind either way."

Clip looks like he appreciates being asked. "You go. But don't get too far ahead."

"I won't." Tom hops onto the first boulder, gripping his phaser tightly in one hand. He moves forward a few more steps and lands on a log that doesn't stay motionless like the other obstacles. It bobs and rolls with his weight, and he spins his arms like a windmill to try to keep his balance. At the last second, he manages to jump onto the next boulder, legs shaking as he throws us a wobbly smile. "Yeah . . . I wouldn't jump on that log."

"I'll try the one next to it," Clip says, following after him. "Stick close together, guys."

"I don't know if I can keep up," Jeremy says in a quiet voice.

Derek pats his shoulder. "Don't worry. I'll hang back with you and Sadie, and we'll take it slow, all right? Thirty minutes is a lot of time. And whoever gets to the island first can start the puzzle." He says it in *such* a nice way. Jeremy's face brightens, and I almost want to hug Derek, except the thought of it makes my stomach all quivery.

So I settle for watching Clip, Caroline, and Iggy take off after Tom, all leaping easily like athletic frogs.

"That's the log that moved," Jeremy says, pointing. "Let's find a way around it."

I scan the swamp and point to a winding route made up of mostly flat rocks. "It looks like there might be different paths to take. That way could be easier, since we'll avoid logs."

"Good thinking, Sadie," Derek says, and I can't stop my big goofy grin. "You guys want me to go first? I'll make sure we have secure footing, and then you follow along?"

"Yeah. Thanks," Jeremy says gratefully. He waits for Derek to move onto the second boulder in the route before stepping gingerly after him.

I bring up the rear, concentrating hard on where I put my feet. The boulders aren't tiny, but they do require a bit of a balancing act. I wave my phaser at Jeremy when he looks back to check on me. "I wonder if we'll even need these. We probably won't be firing lasers, or—"

Yelling breaks out ahead of us, interrupting me.

Derek, Jeremy, and I all freeze on the boulders.

About fifty feet in front of us, Tom, Clip, Caroline, and Iggy are spread out across the swamp, each standing on a different platform. They've got their phasers pointed at the water, and I hear the rapid *ping! ping!* of lasers firing under their shouts.

"What are they aiming at?" Jeremy asks.

Derek looks back at us. "Do you mind if I go ahead and help them?"

"Yeah, we'll be fine," I say, and in a flash, he's hopping nimbly away. When Clip does it, it looks annoying and show-offy, but when Derek does it, he makes it look like a graceful ballet.

"Sadie, look! There's something in the water!" Jeremy cries.

Objects bob in the water near our friends. They move toward Clip, who fires rapidly. Two other objects circle around Caroline, and Tom rushes over to help her shoot lasers at them.

"Come on, we gotta help, too," I say urgently.

Jeremy and I forge ahead as fast as we can. We come to a wide space between two boulders, and Jeremy almost overshoots when he jumps for the second one. His heels catch on the edge of the rock and he cries out, waving his arms so he doesn't fall. His phaser drops into the water with a big splash. After a few tense moments, he finds his footing, sweaty and relieved.

"I'll get your phaser," I offer, and as I grab it, I see a

pair of bright yellow eyes watching me from under the surface. The eyes narrow to evil slits, and then they're joined by another pair of yellow eyes, and then another, until I'm completely surrounded. "Um . . . Jer?!"

Jeremy whirls around as five or six rocky gray-black heads pop through the surface of the water. "Alligators!" he shouts. "Sadie, throw me my phaser!"

Shaking, I toss it to him. The alligators are ambushing my boulder, nostrils flaring and water slipping off their rough faces in sheets. They look like prehistoric monsters made of dark gravel, their eyes watchful and angry, and when they open their enormous mouths, I feel a rush of hot, dank air. Tom never mentioned anything about fighting alligators; this must be yet another adaptation of the arena. It's my turn to mutter to myself, "It's just a game, it's just a game," over and over as the alligators inch closer to me. And then I see that right on the top of their bony, tough skulls, between two ridges of bone, is a target. "Jer! Fire at the top of their heads!"

I point my phaser at the closest target. My laser hits the alligator with a *ping!* and the animal sinks beneath the surface and disappears. Jeremy does the same to two others and is aiming at the third. But it seems like as soon as we get rid of one, two or three more appear.

"There's too many of them!" I cry.

Suddenly, Tom's beside us. "Stay calm, guys!" he says, firing rapidly at the alligators as Jeremy and I gape at him, astonished that he's backtracked all this way to help us. "I'll get this side and you guys get that one. That'll clear your path."

With three of us shooting, the water near me is soon empty of monsters. "Thanks!" I say.

Tom gives me a quick, shy smile. "Least I can do. Y'know, after shoving you like that."

I'm startled to find myself smiling back. "I'm over it."

"Okay, I'm going to go help the others. You guys be careful. Avoid *that* log and *that* log over there. They move like my grandpa's teeth." Tom points at the logs, then takes off.

"Wow. He didn't have to do that," Jeremy says, as we push forward. "I mean, it *is* in his best interest to make sure we're okay, so we all get to the island, but . . ."

"Yeah, I'm confused how to feel about that kid," I admit.

"Well, maybe he's genuinely nice and we'll figure out a way for *all* of us to escape."

By this time, Clip and the others are so far ahead that they're nothing but colorful blurs.

"We're more than halfway!" Jeremy says, and I glance back at the shore where we started the game. I can't believe how far we've come. "We're doing awesome! Let's keep it up!"

"Clip must be on the island by now," I say, shaking my head. "Putting together that silver monkey and making sure the glory is all his. My brother is *so* predictable."

"Well, the team can't win until we get to the island, too. But look! He's not even on it."

I squint ahead and see that Jer's right. The far island is sitting in the middle of the swamp, small and tree-less and there for the taking. But for some reason, my brother isn't on it. He, Iggy, Tom, and the Marshalls are all clustered on a huge boulder, back-to-back, phasers pointed down.

"What are they *doing*?" I ask, puzzled.

And then I see what they're looking at.

Four gigantic alligators break the surface, each at least *twice* the size of all the other monsters we've seen. As Jeremy and I watch, tense and worried, the biggest creature heaves its massive bulk up and out of the swamp, sending a wave of dirty water over our friends as it lunges toward them, mouth open and sharp, white teeth gleaming.

"No!" I cry.

CHAPTER TWENTY-TWO
CLIP

MY BACK IS PRESSED UP AGAINST MY FRIENDS' AS we stand in a circle, facing the onslaught of monsters. Someone is shaking from head to toe—maybe Iggy. "It's gonna be okay, guys," I declare. It's as good a time as any to be a captain, I guess. "These are just bigger, that's all."

"Thanks, Captain Obvious," Caroline says dryly. "But where are *their* targets? There's nothing on top of these ones' heads."

"Tom? Any ideas?" I ask.

"Maybe the tail?" he suggests. "They might turn butt-first, and—"

"I don't think that's the butt!" Iggy yells, as the biggest alligator bursts through the surface with incredible force. It sends a *huge* sheet of dirty swamp water over us, and

Iggy and Caroline scream. But I'm hyper-focused on its stomach, which has a giant target painted across it.

"Eat laser, rock-face!" I shriek, hitting it twice with my red laser beam, and it's like the alligator is blown backward. Its head jerks back as its body is sent flying. But it doesn't vanish the way the smaller alligators did. The monster lands in the swamp with an almighty splash, looking dazed and cross-eyed, then recovers and starts heading toward us again.

Next to me, Tom and Derek fire at another airborne alligator and send it backward.

"The big ones keep coming back!" Caroline shouts, getting down on one knee to aim at the next animal that tries to attack us. "Maybe we have to hit them multiple times?"

Derek swivels, taking out another huge alligator, his face clenched in concentration.

"Bad news, guys." Iggy points at the island we're trying to reach. Swirling around the ferns and grass that surround it are several more enormous alligators. "They're puppy-guarding the goal, and it is *not* fair!" He punctuates his last words with several more lasers.

There's a moment when all the alligators have been blown backward and are recovering, and I take the opportunity to check on my sister and Jeremy. To my surprise, they've caught up to us. They both look scared, but dry as a bone, and I can't help feeling impressed. Those two have a lot more grit than I gave them credit for.

"Nice job, Sadie!" I yell. "Jeremy!"

My sister waves at me, her face brightening for a moment.

"Stay there, okay? Wait until it's safe to get to the island!"

The alligators are coming back. Derek and Caroline are focused on two near them, and Iggy's wiping his sweaty hands on his pants. Tom elbows me gently in the side and points to a particularly nasty-looking alligator.

"Hey, Clip. You wanna take this one out together?" he asks.

I smile. He's been by our side the whole time, working hard, and even backtracked to help Sadie and Jeremy. Definitely not someone to be ashamed of in a crisis. "Teammates?" I say.

"Teammates," he says, grinning as we bump phasers.

As soon as the alligator lifts out of the water, he and I both aim rapidly at the target, firing as many times as we can. This time, when it sinks beneath the surface, it doesn't reappear.

"How many hits was that?" I ask. "Five?"

Tom shrugs. "I thought it was seven!"

"Doesn't matter, just keep fighting!" I roar, taking down another epic beast. I'm in my element. It feels like playing *War of Gods and Men*, except I'm *in* the game. I mean, *we're* in the game. We are mages, warlocks, and monster hunters. We are a kick-butt team, working together, and even though we're under attack? I feel amazing in this circle of friends all defeating evil.

"Okay, good!" Iggy shouts, as two more alligators go down and don't resurface. "Derek, your side is clear. Maybe you should get to the island first and put the statue together!"

"But I'm not good at puzzles," Derek protests. "Shouldn't Sadie or Jeremy—"

"They're too far back!" Caroline yells at her brother. "Just go. Don't worry, we all have to set foot on the island. We'll be there soon to help!"

Reluctantly, Derek hurries across the logs and boulders and lands on the tiny island. There's a stone pedestal in the center that reminds me of Mom's birdbath in our backyard. Scattered around the edges of the island are three heavy-looking pieces of stone. I see Derek lift one that is clearly the monkey's head, with two eyes and two cute little ears.

"No, Derek!" I hear Sadie shout. She and Jeremy have almost reached the island. "That's the third and last piece. Go for the base first! The monkey butt!"

"How do you know?" Derek asks, bewildered, as he stares at the monkey head.

"Because the butt has to go on to that pedestal first!"

Suddenly, the banshee's scratchy voice booms through the arena loudspeakers: "Ten minutes. Ten minutes remaining to put together the statue and return to the starting point."

"Ten minutes!" Iggy, Tom, and Jeremy all chorus in dismay.

"Hurry *up*, Derek!" Caroline screams at her brother.

Flustered, Derek puts the head down and jogs to the other side of the island. He picks up a square-shaped stone, grunting from its weight, and plops it onto the pedestal. "It doesn't fit!"

"That's not the monkey butt!" Jeremy calls. "See how that part has arms?"

"Derek, how hard is it to put together three pieces of a monkey?" Caroline shrieks.

"I'm panicking, okay?!" Derek screams back, his face pink with effort as he tries to jam the monkey body on *top* of the monkey head.

"Oh, boy," I mutter. Derek hates time-based

challenges. He's great at games—he's got a solid and strategic brain—but show the kid a timer and he loses his cool. As my friends continue firing at the alligators, I realize the clear path is now right in front of me and Sadie. "Jer, hop on this boulder and take my spot. Help Iggy and Tom and Caro get these last monsters, okay?"

Jeremy nods eagerly.

I catch my sister's eye. "Hey. You wanna go put that monkey together?"

Sadie grins from ear to ear, and we hop along the boulders until we reach a very sweaty and stressed-out Derek. "Dude, go help everyone else. We'll take care of this," I say, clapping him on the back, and he leaps into the alligator action with relief.

Sadie sprints across the island for the third stone piece. It's definitely the monkey butt because it has a long curling tail on the back. She grits her teeth under its weight, and I hurry over to help. Together, we carry it to the pedestal, which has a square indentation on the top.

"Here, maybe turn it this way," I suggest, and we shift around until the bottom of the stone piece lines up with the pedestal. It locks into place with a satisfying click.

"We got this!" Sadie exclaims.

Together, she and I lift the monkey's body. "Nice! Just a few more steps!" I say, panting.

"Wait, I think the monkey is supposed to be facing out. Toward the swamp."

"You're right," I agree, and we set the piece on top with the monkey stomach facing out. "Last one! The head! Want to do the honors?"

Sadie looks at me, surprised, and shakes her head. "Let's do it together," she says, her eyes bright, and I can't help grinning.

As one, we lift the head, grunting as we place it on top of the statue. It clicks into place, and a green light flickers on, lighting up the entire thing, monkey and pedestal together. A loud mechanical whirring sounds out across the swamp, and we turn to see all of the wooden bridges slowly lowering to form one long, sturdy bridge that leads from the island back to shore. Sadie and I slap a high ten, both beaming from ear to ear.

"Yesssss!" Sadie shouts.

"Team Chuuuuuu!" I roar, beating my chest gorilla-style.

"You guys did it!" Derek shouts, and all of our friends cheer. They've taken out every single alligator, and now they hop across the quiet, empty swamp to join us on the island.

"Man, it was so inspiring watching you two work together," Caroline jokes, jabbing Derek in the ribs. "Nice to see people who actually know what they're doing."

"Sadie figured out which way the monkey was supposed to be facing," I say.

"And Clip provided the muscle," my sister adds.

"I gotta hand it to you, little Chu," I tell her. "You're pretty dang good at this."

She flips her ponytail over her shoulder, trying not to look too pleased. "I've been trying to tell you all along. Clip Chu might be the laser tag master, but Sadie Chu's not half-bad."

"Laser tag *master*!" I say, grinning. "I like the sound of that."

"Yo, laser tag master, we got, like . . . single-digit

minutes to haul this thing back," Iggy interrupts, pointing at the monkey. "And it looks mad heavy."

"I'll help you take the first leg," Tom offers, and together he and Iggy lift the statue.

Carrying the monkey back across the swamp is definitely tricky and takes a lot of teamwork, even with a solid bridge to cross and no alligators in the way. The statue is bulky and hard to hold on to, so we're all extra careful when we pass it to each other. It's like an awkward kind of relay race. But we manage until finally we're all back on the shore. We put the monkey down, everyone breathing hard. The banshee is nowhere to be seen, but it's just as well.

Jeremy drops to his knees and hugs the ground. "Thank Gandalf. I could kiss this dirt."

"Don't," Sadie advises. "It's probably gross gym mats that tons of kids have sweated on."

"Way to ruin the moment, Sadie," Derek jokes, looking thrilled to be back on solid ground himself. He and Iggy high-five each other, and then they hug Caroline.

"Well, we did it!" I say triumphantly. "We beat every single battleground."

Sadie cups a hand around one ear. "Excuse me. You said *we*?"

I give her a light shove. "Yes, nerd. I said *we*. No way one kid could have done all that solo." I look across the swamp, with its boulders and logs scattered on either side of the long wooden bridge, and imagine being ambushed by a dozen alligators and having to carry that statue back alone. "We made a good team. And now we're done. Right?"

"Yeah. What happens now?" Jeremy asks, as everybody turns to look at Tom.

Caroline frowns. "Tom? Where are you going?"

Tom has walked away a few steps, facing the trees. And when he turns back to us, he's hugging his phaser to his chest and his giant bug eyes are full of tears. "I'm sorry," he says in a choked voice. "I just . . . I never thought I would get here again, to this moment. To victory. You know when you really want something to happen for years? And it finally does, and you're thrilled, but like . . . it feels weird and unreal at the same time?"

I think of how I climbed the ranks of my soccer team, bit by painful bit, and nod.

Sadie's nodding, too, and I wonder if she's thinking about school.

"And I really ended up liking you guys. You know?" Tom wipes his wet face, laughing. "I wish . . . I wish we could all be friends. And hang out and watch movies and stuff."

"Of course we can!" Caroline says kindly, putting an arm around him.

Derek pats his shoulder, too. "We *are* friends. I mean, we just fought a horde of alligators together, didn't we?"

Tom exhales. "I don't think you guys are gonna want to be friends when I tell you . . ."

"That there has to be one person left behind in the game?" Sadie finishes, and he stares at her in shock. "Yeah, we suspected that back when you were talking about those other kids. You said you weren't going to be the one who *has* to stay behind this time."

"I . . . I . . ." he stammers, then hangs his head, tears spilling down his face.

"You were planning to leave one of us behind," Iggy adds, but without any anger in his voice. "Look, dude, you were stuck for a long time and it did things to you."

"No. It doesn't make it okay," Tom says fiercely. "Just because I had the bad luck to be trapped in the game . . . and, like, get messed up by it, doesn't make it okay that I wanted this to happen to anyone else. I don't want any of you to get stuck." He looks at us, his face desperately sad. "You're my friends now.

And . . . I think it's only right if you guys go, and I stay behind."

Everyone starts talking at once.

"No, Tom! You shouldn't have to stay even longer!" Derek argues.

"That's not fair!" Caroline says. "You've been in here for years already!"

Jeremy shakes his head. "No way, we're not leaving anyone behind."

"There's gotta be some kind of loophole or something!" Sadie cries.

Tom sighs. "There's no loophole. When those kids and I won, everybody walked out that glowing door in one big group. But instead of getting back to the real world, we got pulled back into this arena. The Swamp of Despair." He swipes his sleeve across his face. "We did it over and over. They were mad because they thought I'd tricked them, and there *was* no escape. But then they decided to try leaving more slowly, one by one, and that worked."

"And then when it came down to the last few people . . ." Iggy prompts.

"The last two guys looked at each other and said sorry. And then they ran out on me."

Derek blows out a breath. "Unbelievable!"

"I don't blame them, honestly," Tom says. "I mean, being stuck in here sucks. I would know . . . and I *was* thinking of doing the same thing to them. But they left before I could, and when I tried to go, I ended up back in the In-Between. Right where I started. I didn't play the game for a couple of weeks after that. I just sat and cried."

"So that's how you figured out there's always gotta be one person stuck inside," Sadie says quietly, putting a hand on Tom's shoulder.

He gives her a shaky smile. "Now you know why I'm so jittery and intense. It was just so hard, and I didn't want that to happen to me again. But now," he adds, looking around at everyone, "I don't want it to happen to any of you, either."

A voice speaks up. "And it's not going to."

We all turn to see Mardella Blackwood stepping out of the familiar glowing door.

"MOM?" TOM WHISPERS.

Mardella has clearly been crying, too. "Hi, Tommy," she says softly, and opens her arms.

Tom stares at her for a moment, and then runs right into her hug. They stand very still for a long moment, and we can hear Tom's muffled sobs against her shoulder. Iggy, Jeremy, and I are all openly crying, and I even catch Clip wiping away tears.

Finally, Mardella looks at us, her arms still around her son. She's wearing the same outfit as the day Clip, Jeremy, and I met her: a long purple dress and the necklace with the gingerbread house charm. "I want to thank you all for helping Tom," she says. "I have to admit, I was starting to lose hope. I tried everything to save him: reprogramming the game, overriding the system, coding in escape routes. But nothing ever worked, except recruiting kids to team up with him."

"You mean *luring* kids," I correct her.

"You're right, Sadie. Luring kids." She kisses the top of Tom's head. "I wasn't the best mom before Tom got stuck, but even I was willing to do anything—sacrifice *anything*, even other people's children—to get my boy out. When that last group of players left him behind, I was just as devastated as Tom. But you kids seem different. You care about him."

"I care about them, too, Mom," Tom tells her. "I want them to escape."

"I know. Luellen and I were watching the whole thing in the control room," Mardella says, laughing at our shocked expressions. "Yes, I know my sister is here. I ran into her last week, disguised as a staff member, and we had a long talk. We made up, in a way. It'll be a long time before she completely forgives me, but this will be my first olive branch."

"Why didn't she tell me?" Tom asks, stunned.

Mardella runs a hand over his hair. "Didn't want you to get distracted, I guess."

"What do you mean by olive branch?" Clip asks. "Have you figured out a way to get everybody out?"

"No, I have not. Lu's a brilliant game designer, and these worlds she created . . ." Her eyes take in the swamp, from the vines to the trees to the boulders. "They took on a life of their own, in a way my own games never have or will. I hate to admit it, but she's better than me."

"Is she watching us right now?" Tom asks.

Mardella chuckles. "You bet she is, and probably recording this speech. And if anyone needed proof that *she* was the one who designed this arena . . ." She points to the monkey statue on the ground. "She designed that to look like Chimper, the stuffed animal she had when she was little. Even after all these years, I remember him. She wouldn't go anywhere without him."

"Chimper!" Tom exclaims. "You gave him to me."

"You never threw him away?" Caroline asks, amazed.

"No. The truth is, I missed my sister. Deep down, I wanted to make things right with her, but I tried to stay angry and refuse her attempts to make up so my shame wouldn't hurt so much. The weird thing about anger, though, is it fades with time. So I kept Chimper for my child, as a piece of the sister I lost." Mardella looks at Tom with so much love in her eyes that I start tearing up again, and I hear Jeremy and Iggy sniffle. "I want to make up for everything I've done. I wasn't a great mom to you, Tommy, and I wasn't a great sister to Luellen. So if anyone's going to be left in the game, it will be me. I will stay behind, and you kids leave."

We all look at each other, wide-eyed.

"What? Really?" Clip demands.

Mardella nods. "I stole my sister's idea. I was the one who started all of this, and it's only right that I should be the one taking the punishment. Not my boy."

"Why didn't you ever take his place before?" Jeremy asks.

"Believe me, I tried, but for some reason, it's harder for grown-ups to get inside the game. Together, Luellen and I finally figured out a way to tinker with the code. I guess all it took was teamwork." Mardella strokes Tom's hair. "And now that I'm in, I don't want my son or any of you innocent kids here. When it comes right down to it, I couldn't live with myself."

Tom nods. "That's how I feel. I was so ready to leave them behind in the game. Especially Clip," he adds, and my brother grins and rolls his eyes. "But when the time came, I imagined what it would be like, knowing I'd doomed someone else. And I couldn't do it."

I shift my weight from one foot to the other. What Mardella's saying makes sense—she *did* steal Luellen's game and take all the credit for it. But it still doesn't feel right that someone, *anyone*, is going to stay trapped in this game. "Isn't there some other way?" I ask.

She smiles. "Luellen's been working hard on the outside, trying to get Tom out, and she's getting close. If anyone can find a loophole for me, it's her. Meanwhile, I plan to fiddle with the coding inside the game. I'm confident we'll find a way eventually."

"Are you?" Tom asks quietly.

"Yes." Mardella puts a hand on either side of his face. "I promise we will be together again. And I'm going to be around for you this time. I love you so much, Tommy."

"I love you, too, Mom." He hugs her tightly.

Mardella nods at us over the top of his head. "You guys can go. You'll find yourselves back in the arena—the *real* arena, with the gym mats and the ropes and the twisty slide. No simulation. Take care of yourselves . . . and thank you again."

But nobody moves a muscle, and I can see from the looks on everyone's faces that they're thinking the same thing I am. Clip, of course, is the one to speak for us all. "We want Tom to leave first," he says, and the boy turns to look at him, surprised. "He deserves it."

"Really?" Tom asks gratefully.

We all nod.

Tom shakes Iggy's and Derek's hands, then hugs me, Jer, and Caroline. And then he faces my brother. "It was a real honor to be on your team, Clip," he says.

"*Our* team," Clip corrects him, and they shake hands, beaming at each other.

Tom turns back to his mom, who gives him a tearful smile. "I promise Aunt Lu and I are going to get you out. Just wait and see."

"I know you will," Mardella says softly.

He takes a deep breath, his phaser trembling in his shaking hands. "Here goes nothing," he says, and then he marches out of the glowing door and disappears.

"You next," Clip says to the Marshall twins, who follow Tom out with their arms slung over each other's shoulders. "Then you, Iggy."

"Whew, I really thought we were gonna be stuck in here for all eternity. Glad I was wrong," Iggy says, vanishing after Derek and Caroline.

"You next, Jer," I say, squeezing my best friend's shoulder. "I mean, Mithrandir."

Jeremy gives me a jellyfish fist bump. "See you on the other side, Samwise."

And then it's just Clip and me, standing in front of the glowing door. I look back at Mardella. "Are you going to be okay in here by yourself?" I ask.

She smiles. "I think so. But I do wish I had a sibling with me, the way you two have each other. Luellen told me about you guys, and how you remind her a little of us."

My brother and I look at each other sheepishly. "Yeah. I guess we do fight a lot," I admit. "But it actually has been fun being on the same team. Team Chu, like you said back there."

Clip's eyebrows almost touch his hairline. "Yeah?" He ruffles my hair, which he knows I *hate*. "Aw, look at that. My little sister thinks I'm not an arrogant bighead anymore."

"Well, I wouldn't go *that* far," I say, smoothing my ponytail. "But this was, like, the *ultimate* game of laser tag. And you weren't completely horrible all the time."

"Wow, I feel special." He grins and scratches his head. "This whole thing has been ridiculous. First the Deadly Cliffs. Feeding that dragon and firing giant eggs into its mouth . . ."

I laugh, remembering how everyone freaked out and ran up the cliff, thinking the dragon was chasing us when it was only following us to the roc's nest. "And then in the Haunted Castle, when you screamed, 'THE KNIGHTS ARE ALIVE!' Jeremy nearly peed himself," I say, and he and Mardella both laugh. "You put up a good fight against the knights."

"You weren't so bad yourself in the Mad Scientist's Lab, solving all those riddles. If it hadn't been for you and Jeremy, it would have taken us a lot longer."

"And then that," I say, pointing at the stone monkey statue. "We did that together."

"I guess we do make a pretty good team, huh?" Clip says. "That is, when you're not yelling at me for stealing all the glory."

"And when *you're* not talking down to *me* and treating me like I'm five." For some reason, my eyes are tearing up again. I guess it's because we never talk to each other like this. He makes fun of me and I criticize him, and Grandma spoils him and scolds me, and we're always at odds with each other. "You know, we've never had a single thing in common except . . ."

"Laser tag?"

"Well, yeah. But I was *going* to say . . . except being the Chu siblings. There's only two of us, and no one else in the world gets what it's like to be us." I take a deep breath. "So before we go back out there . . . I'm sorry for insulting you so much. You're a good leader."

He looks taken aback. "Okay. Well. I'm sorry I underestimated you. You're an okay laser tag player, when it comes down to it. A *good* player, even. I'm, uh . . ." He scuffs his sneaker on the ground. "I'm proud of you."

"Man, I wish I was recording this right now!" I exclaim, blinking away tears.

Mardella's gentle voice breaks into our conversation. "I'm curious. Let's say you *did* have to choose one person to stay, and you two were the last ones. What would you have done?"

Clip doesn't even hesitate. "I would have pushed Sadie out the door. I got her and everyone else into this mess. Tom brought me in here, but I didn't have to bring them, too."

I swallow hard, thinking of Clip with big black bug eyes, trapped in the simulation for years like Tom. I imagine going home to Mom and Dad and seeing my brother's room stay empty. I picture Grandma cooking all of his favorite meals only to find out he's never coming back. "You'd sacrifice yourself for me?" I ask, staring at him.

"You're my sister." His eyes are mysteriously shiny, like they're wet or something. He holds out his arms, and I dodge him. "Will you stop being such a weirdo? I just want a hug."

"You *what?*" I sputter.

This is too much for me. Clip is the kind of person who *hates* hugs and kisses, and he won't let Mom do more than wrap an arm around him for a few seconds before he squirms away. Grandma's the only person who's allowed to fully hug him, and even then—as Dad likes to joke—Clip gets rigor mortis. But here is my brother, standing in front of me with his arms wide-open. So I do the only sane thing I can: burst into tears and hug him.

"I wouldn't leave you behind, stupid," I sob. "Who

would make fun of me when I'm playing video games? Who would I yell at for being loud when they're playing *War of Gods and Men*? Who would help me look for fat noodles when Grandma makes pho?" Our grandmother uses a brand of noodle that's cut skinny, but sometimes there's a wide one that gets missed. Clip and I always hunt for them in our bowls because Mom says they're lucky.

"Sadie . . ." he says, trying to break in.

"And To-f-fu!" I'm full-on bawling by this point. "Who would help me walk him and feed him table scraps? You couldn't abandon poor Tofu; that would be a crime!"

Clip pats my back gingerly and tries to dislodge me. "Come on, sis, let go. You're hurting me," he complains, but I only tighten my hug around his middle. "Sadie! Stop!"

Mardella laughs, and I let go, having forgotten she was there. Tears stream down her face as she looks at us. "You two really love each other, huh?"

"Ew," Clip mutters, and I smack his arm.

Mardella's smile is the saddest one I've ever seen. "Luellen never liked to admit that, either. She didn't like anything touchy-feely, but I knew she loved me. And I loved her, too. *Love* her, no matter what's happened between us. You're right about what you said, Sadie: that when you have siblings, no one else in the world knows what it's like to be one of you."

I bite my lip, watching her struggle for control. I don't think I've ever seen a grown-up cry before, except when my mom watches Pixar movies.

"Siblings grow up together. They have inside jokes, secret languages, and codes only they understand. It's different from any other bond in the world. So thanks for reminding me about that. I had forgotten." Mardella walks back over to the stone monkey and kneels beside it, running her hand tenderly over its head. "This game started with two sisters who couldn't find their way back to each other. And I'm glad it's going to end with two siblings who finally see each other's worth. Go on, now. Leave . . . and take care of each other, always."

"Come on, nerd," Clip says, putting an arm around my shoulders.

"Let's go home, dummy," I say, putting my arm around his waist.

And we walk out the door together, back into the real world.

CHAPTER TWENTY-FOUR
CLIP

GRANDMA POKES HER HEAD INTO MY ROOM. "Clip-ah, come downstairs. I need you."

"For what, Grandma?" I ask, keeping my eyes on my computer screen. It's Wednesday afternoon and the soccer team has the whole day off from volunteering, so of course I decided to launch an attack on the enemy kingdom in *War of Gods and Men.* Iggy, Derek, and I have all leveled up to Level 85, Woodland Warlocks, which means we get to have animal familiars, and my polar bear and I are currently fending off orcs while Iggy and Derek storm their castle.

"I need you," Grandma repeats. "Right now."

An orc swipes at me with its poisoned blade. "This really isn't a good time," I say, as my warlock character ducks. Jellybean, my polar bear, gives a ferocious roar and body-slams the orc.

"Clip!"

"Okay, okay," I say, sighing. I speak into the microphone attached to my headset. "Sorry, guys, my grandma needs me downstairs."

"Right now?" Iggy squawks. "But Derek and I just got to the East Tower!"

"Have Jeremy cover you. I mean . . . Mithrandir."

Jeremy's voice comes through the headset loud and clear, and I can tell he's grinning. "I would be happy to do that, Warlock Clip! Just give me a second," he says, and within moments, a handsome, bearded Black mage riding a giant pink pig appears on-screen. He gives two thumbs-up and proceeds to fire punching spells at, like, twelve orcs in rapid succession.

"Clip! Now!" Grandma yells from the stairs.

Reluctantly, I tear my eyes from the screen and follow her voice down to the kitchen.

My sister's at the table, stirring so much sugar into her lemonade, it makes my teeth hurt. "How come I haven't heard you yell and scream all morning?" she asks, rubbing Tofu's back with her foot. Our dog is passed out under the table, snoring loudly.

"Because I've got this castle ambush *handled*, that's why. Jeremy's taking over for me."

"He still can't believe you guys are letting him play with you," Sadie says.

I shrug. "Now that I've seen what he can do at laser tag, I figured why not? He might be a good ally to have on *War of Gods and Men*." I turn to our grandmother, who points at the sink to tell me to wash my hands. "What do you need me for, Grandma?"

"You're helping me roll chả giò today," she replies. She takes out a package of rice paper and starts peeling off thin square sheets, laying them on the clean kitchen counters.

"But Sadie's better at this; can't she—" I start to protest.

"No. *You* are helping me today."

That's the kind of tone Sadie and I are never, *ever* supposed to argue with, so I sigh and wash my hands. Grandma pulls over this giant tub of ground pork mixed with diced shrimp, skinny clear noodles, beaten eggs, and grated carrots, which she seasons with pepper and fish sauce. She turns the rice paper so it looks like a diamond, and then points to the bottom edge.

"You put a spoon of the meat . . . here," she says, watching as I grudgingly obey. "Not too much. Then fold in the sides. Now roll it up from the bottom. Nice and tight . . . and then seal it with a wet fingertip. Good! One down, four dozen to go."

"Four dozen!" I almost scream.

"And then after we do the four dozen, *you* will fry them," Grandma says, indicating a pan full of oil ready to be heated. "We are going to have a nice lunch today."

Chả giò is one of my favorite things to eat. I love wrapping the crunchy egg rolls in lettuce and dipping them into fish sauce, or eating them over cool noodles with crispy sliced cucumber. But *making* them is a whole other story, because after what feels like *hours*, I've only rolled . . . three. "Why does Vietnamese food take so long to make?" I grumble.

"Because it's worth it. You know that." In the same amount of time, Grandma has rolled a full dozen. "Maybe now you'll appreciate Bà ngoại more, ha?" She elbows me in the ribs and winks at Sadie, who leans against the fridge, drinking lemonade and watching me suffer.

"Why doesn't Sadie have to help?" I complain, struggling with an overstuffed roll.

"She knows how to make these. She helps me every other time."

Finally, when we've got about two and a half dozen egg rolls—with all the lumpy, weird-shaped ones being mine, of course—Grandma takes pity on me and sets me up at the frying pan. I plop the egg rolls into the hot oil with chopsticks, slowly turning them so they get brown.

Sadie comes over to watch. "Turn down the heat

a little so that doesn't happen," she advises, as the oil splatters my hand and I yelp.

"Look who knows everything," I say, but I do as she suggests and it works.

"So, do you think Mardella got out?"

I look at her. "I hope so. I could call the arena *again*, but I don't want to look weird and obsessed. I did just call them two days ago." Since our Friday night laser tag marathon, none of us have felt like going back to the Blackwood Gaming Arena. At least, not yet.

"It's kind of strange that Tom and Luellen weren't there when you called. You'd think they would spend all their time working on getting her out. I wish we'd gotten Tom's number."

"Maybe they're working on it somewhere else. Or maybe they—" My phone vibrates, interrupting me. "Oh, whoa. It's the arena calling! Grandma, I have to take this!"

"Clip-ah," my grandmother says disapprovingly.

"It's okay, I'll take over," Sadie offers, snatching the chopsticks from me. Tofu hustles over and presses his fluffy yellow bulk against her legs, wide awake now that the food's almost done cooking. He and I are definitely related.

"Hello?" I say breathlessly into the phone.

A woman's voice answers, crisp and businesslike. "Hello, this is Naima Dennis calling from the Blackwood Gaming Arena. May I speak to Clip Chu, please?"

"This is him!" I exclaim, whispering, "It's the COO," to Sadie.

"This is *he*," she whispers back, like the grammar nerd she is.

"Great," Ms. Dennis says. "I'm assuming your sister, Sadie Chu, is also there? I'm calling to invite you both back to the arena. Don't worry, you're not in trouble. It's a surprise, and it won't take very long. When would you both be available to come in?"

I cover my phone with my free hand and relay all this excitedly to Sadie, whose eyes grow as round as saucers. "Tonight!" she whispers.

"How does tonight work?" I ask Ms. Dennis.

"Fine for me, but you'd be doing me a big favor if you reached out to the following people to see if they're free, too." I hear her clicking away on a keyboard. "Let's see . . . Ignacio Morales, Derek Marshall, Caroline Marshall, and Jeremy 'Mithrandir' Thomas." She struggles a little with the word *Mithrandir*, and I snicker. Jeremy must have typed that into the system when we were setting up our player barcodes. "Your whole group has been invited back."

"Okay," I say, shoving my hand in front of Sadie's frantic face as she jumps and mouths, *What? What?!* "I can reach out to those people. And you can't tell us any more than that?"

"Nope. Just call me back at this number and let me know if all of you can come, okay?"

"Okay! Bye!" I practically shout into the phone, and fill Sadie in on everything she said. "It's gotta be Mardella, right? Maybe Tom and Luellen got her out, and they want to throw us a party or something with cake and confetti and—"

"Or maybe they need our help," Sadie says, her face suddenly serious. "Maybe they need us to get back into the game, and—"

"Don't even *joke* about that," I tell her. I turn to our grandmother. "Grandma, would you mind watching the frying pan while Sadie and I video chat our friends? It'll be real quick, I swear! And when I come back, I'll roll a dozen more egg rolls!"

"You might not be done until Christmas," Grandma says dryly. "Fine. Go, go."

In the living room, Sadie and I crowd together on the couch as I send a video chat request to everybody. Iggy's the first one to appear, and then Jeremy and Caroline.

"Where's Derek?" I ask.

"He's here," Caroline says, tilting her phone so we can

see Derek with his eyes glued to his computer. On the screen, I see that he's still busy with the orc castle. "He's listening."

Quickly, I explain about Ms. Dennis's invitation.

"It's gotta be Tom," Derek says, still clicking furiously away at his keyboard. "Maybe he wants to show us something. Maybe they renamed the arena in our honor."

"All of us?" Iggy asks, raising his eyebrows. "I think the Iggy Derek Caroline Sadie Jeremy Clip Gaming Arena is gonna be quite a mouthful."

"Hey, why is my name last?" I complain.

"Okay, fine, the Clip Iggy Derek Car—"

"So can you guys come or what?" Sadie breaks in, bouncing in her seat.

One by one, everybody nods, including Derek when Caroline points the camera at him.

"All right, so how's eight p.m.?" I suggest. "Team Chu will reconvene in the lobby of the Blackwood Gaming Arena. See you all there, and don't be late!"

The lobby is packed as always when we arrive. There's a huge long line of kids waiting for their pizza and milkshakes, and several families scanning their barcodes into the system. But despite how busy it is, Naima Dennis sees us immediately from where she's standing behind the front desk. She grins, holds a microphone to her mouth, and starts speaking into it. Her voice echoes from all the speakers in the lobby and farther back in the arena.

"Good evening, gamers, and happy Wednesday! May I please direct your attention to the group of kids who just walked in the door?"

The whole lobby quiets down, and everyone turns to us curiously.

"Why am I asking you to look at them?" Ms. Dennis asks. "Because I wanted to introduce you to the brand-new ultimate laser tag champions of the Blackwood Gaming Arena!"

Someone starts clapping, setting off a chain reaction of applause and whistles. I can clearly hear a kid groan, "Aw, *man*! I wanted to get number one on the leaderboard tonight."

"The leaderboard," I mutter, and hustle forward to look at the screen. What I see makes my jaw drop. The top slot has six names squeezed into it. *Our* names. "Guys! Look, it's us!"

"Yaaaaaaaaaas!" Iggy and Caroline yell.

"We did it!" Jeremy says, hugging a beaming Sadie.

Derek slaps me a high five. "This is amazing!"

"So what, are we getting on that show?!" Sadie demands, looking at me.

I gape at her, having forgotten about the *War of Gods and Men* show. "Oh my god, you're right! We're gonna be on TV!" I feel a little faint. I think back to what Tom said in the Swamp of Despair, when we beat the game, about how you want something to happen so badly that it feels a little weird when it *does*. "Let's get some confirmation from Ms. Dennis first."

The COO of the Blackwood Gaming Arena is waving us over. "Come on into the staff room with me, guys," she says, leading us around the front desk into a space with a long wooden table and a bunch of wheeled chairs. She gestures for us all to sit down.

"Are we gonna be on the show?" Jeremy asks her, wasting no time whatsoever.

"And how did we win if we didn't find the last two Brass Keys?" Sadie adds.

Ms. Dennis laughs. "Now hold on," she says, closing the meeting room door. In her hands, she has a slightly bulky manila envelope. "Okay. So this past weekend, my staff member Luellen took me aside and told me that the six of you absolutely *dominated* at laser tag on Friday. Also, she dropped the bombshell that she's secretly Mardella's sister and introduced me to her nephew, Tom.

He also raved about how amazing you all were. Sweet kid." She scratches her head. "Though I still have *no* idea why Mardella hid the fact that she had family."

I exchange glances with my friends. It sounds like Luellen didn't tell her Tom had been stuck in the game. But I kind of get why. I mean, who would believe her aside from us? "So . . . how did they tell you we dominated, exactly?" I ask.

"They told me your team played six consecutive games and won every single one. *Crushed* was the word that Tom used, I believe," Ms. Dennis tells us. "I wish I hadn't chosen to take that night off, or I would have been here to witness your incredible victory! But anyway, Luellen and Tom decided that such a *ridiculous* accomplishment—another word Tom used—was more than worthy of the points you would have gotten for finding the Brass Keys. So congrats!"

My friends and I all cheer. In that moment, keys don't matter, brass or not, real or not. We all get what this is about: Luellen and Tom thanking us for helping them.

"So, in answer to your question," Ms. Dennis continues, looking at Jeremy, "yes, as the champions, you all will be eligible for spots on the *War of Gods and Men* TV show."

We all cheer again, and I feel like I could literally fly around the arena, Superman-style. This is *everything* I've ever wanted: everyone in school seeing my face in their living rooms. And now I get to do it with my sister and our friends.

"You typed your addresses into the system when you first registered here, so we will be mailing you the information, including waivers and forms for your parents to sign," Ms. Dennis says. "You should get those next week. But right now, Luellen and Tom have asked me to give you *this* and have you read what's inside. In private. Any other questions before I leave you to it?" She points to the sealed manila envelope on the table.

"No, I don't think so," I say, looking around at the group.

"Great! Come on out when you're done and enjoy some pizza and milkshakes. On the house," she says, winking, and then she leaves and closes the door.

We all start talking at once.

"Free pizza, Jer!" Sadie's exclaiming. "And milkshakes!"

Caroline smirks. "Did you see those kids' faces when they heard we were the champs?"

"Do you think we'll have warlock costumes on the show?" Derek asks excitedly.

"Where do you think they'll film? Australia?!" Iggy adds.

"Hang on, guys, let's see what Tom and Luellen left us," Jeremy suggests, reaching for the manila envelope.

Everyone falls silent and watches as he rips it and shakes out the contents.

The first thing to emerge is a silver chain necklace with a gingerbread house charm.

The second thing is a *second* silver chain necklace with a gingerbread house charm.

And the third thing is a note, typed and printed.

"Guys!" Sadie says in a choked voice, pointing at the two necklaces. "Mardella was wearing hers when Clip and I left her in the game. If it's here with us, on the table . . ."

"That means she got out!" Caroline and Jeremy say at the same time.

"I knew it!" I say, pumping my fist. "I knew they would rescue her. But where are they? Why aren't any of them here to explain in person?"

Jeremy's scanning the note. "It's from Tom!" he says, and reads it aloud.

DEAR DRAGON-FEEDING, ZOMBIE-KNIGHT-FIGHTING,
ALLIGATOR-ATTACKING CREW,

IF YOU ARE READING THIS, I AM ON A SANDY BEACH
SOMEWHERE WITH PALM TREES AND SUNSCREEN
AND A GLASS OF OJ WITH AN UMBRELLA IN IT,
AND YOU SHOULD BE REALLY JEALOUS. ESPECIALLY

BECAUSE I DON'T SEE ANY BANSHEES OR HEDGE
MAZES OR ROCS . . . AT LEAST, NOT RIGHT NOW.

AUNT LU AND I GOT MOM OUT ON SUNDAY NIGHT.
THERE WAS A LOT OF CRYING. (LIKE, A LOT OF
CRYING.) WE DIDN'T SLEEP ALL WEEKEND AFTER YOU
GUYS LEFT, AND WORKED AROUND THE CLOCK ON
THE CODING AUNT LU HAD BEEN TINKERING WITH.
SOMEHOW WHATEVER SHE WAS DOING ON THE OUTSIDE,
ADDED TO WHATEVER MOM WAS DOING ON THE INSIDE,
MADE IT ALL WORK.

AND WHEN MOM WALKED OUT THE DOOR, SHE
WALKED OUT THE DOOR. SAFE AND SOUND. AND
SHE WAS SO HAPPY, SHE TOOK ME AND AUNT LU ON
VACATION THE NEXT DAY.

IT'S ALL THANKS TO YOU GUYS. BEING THE ARENA
DESIGNER'S NEPHEW HAS SOME PERKS, AND I TOLD
THE SNACK BAR PEOPLE TO GIVE YOU FREE MILKSHAKES
AND PIZZA EVERY TIME YOU WALK IN THE DOOR. AND
OF COURSE MOM AND AUNT LU HAVE ALREADY TALKED
TO THEIR PEOPLE AT JCD UNIVERSAL ABOUT HAVING
YOU GUYS ON THE SHOW. I MIGHT COME VISIT YOU ON
THE SET, IF THAT'S OK?!!!

OH, YEAH, BEFORE I FORGET. MOM HELPED ME SET
UP A NEW EMAIL ADDRESS. IT'S TOM@BLACKWOOD
GAMINGARENA.LASERTAG. MAYBE WHEN I'M BACK IN

TOWN, WE CAN PLAY SOMETHING ELSE THAT'S A
LITTLE LESS HIGH STAKES . . . LIKE PICTIONARY.

ANYWAY, THANKS, YOU GUYS. I'LL SEE YOU WHEN
WE'RE ALL BACK FROM VACATION.

YOUR FRIEND,
TOM

There is barely a dry eye in the room when Jeremy finishes reading, his voice all choked up. Iggy's bawling, and
Sadie's wiping her eyes on her sleeve. We all sit there for
a minute, just looking at each other and at the necklaces
and the note left by our laser tag teammate. Our *friend*.

"I knew there'd be a happy ending," Derek says, all
misty-eyed.

"I guess we can keep these necklaces," Sadie says,
taking one of the gingerbread house charms in her hand.
"Who wants the other one?"

Derek, Caroline, and I all shake our heads, and Iggy
jokes, "It doesn't go with any of my outfits," so Jeremy
shrugs and puts the silver chain around his neck, grinning.

"Let's get our free pizza and milkshakes, I guess," I say.

We all file out of the meeting room, and on our way to
the food counter, a couple of high school staff members
greet us.

"Welcome to the arena! Are you guys here to play laser tag?" one of them asks, smiling.

Everyone exchanges glances, grinning.

"Ummmmm, maybe not," Sadie says, fingering the charm around her neck.

"We could use something a little calmer. Maybe Skee-Ball?" Caroline suggests. "The holes are too small for us to get stuck in."

"Mini-golf?" Derek adds. "There's no way we can fall down one of *those* holes, either."

"How about Spider Stompin'?" Iggy suggests, pointing at the arcade, where there's a sort of whack-a-mole-like game where you jump on fuzzy purple spiders as they pop up. "I don't think those spiders have targets for us to fire at, do you?"

And then we all start cracking up. Like, *cracking up*. Tears running down our faces, stomachs hurting. The staff members look at us like we've all completely lost our marbles and inch away, and we continue making our way over to the snack bar.

I nudge Sadie, who's walking next to me at the back of the group. "Hey, so how about a game of *Mario-Kart* later? That seems safe," I joke, pointing at the game consoles in the lobby.

"As long as I can be—"

"Yoshi, I know, I know. Your favorite."

She raises her eyebrows at me. "So what does this mean? Are we best friends now?"

I snort. "You *wish* you were cool enough to be friends with *me*."

Sadie aims a playful kick at my shins, and I dodge it.

"I keep thinking about what Mardella said to us on Friday," I admit. "And I'm thinking maybe we don't need to be best friends. We just need to . . . I dunno, appreciate each other a little bit more? You know? Like, you respect me."

"And *you* respect *me*?" Sadie asks sassily.

"Maybe," I say, and my sister rolls her eyes, smiling. "Yeah. And I respect you."

Because maybe all it takes to be better siblings is to fight a giant bird of prey or dodge knights or put together the statue of a silver monkey while trying not to fall into a swamp.

"So we're a team?" Sadie asks.

"We're a team," I reply.

We look at each other, grinning.

"Team Chuuuuuuuuu!" we say together.

ACKNOWLEDGMENTS

If you told ten-year-old Julie Dao that a couple of decades later, she would grow up to write a middle-grade adventure novel partly inspired by her favorite Nickelodeon shows (hello, *Legends of the Hidden Temple*, *Double Dare*, and *GUTS*), she would flip out. I can tell you that grown-up Julie Dao is flipping out! And there are a few very important key players to thank.

As always, the first thanks go to my family near and far, especially Mom: You've filled our home with so much love and delicious food throughout the years, and the meals in *Team Chu and the Battle of Blackwood Arena* are a tribute to your (certified yummy) cooking. Jon and Justin: Our annual escape room, *Mario Party*, and board game marathons are the stuff of legends, as are our epic Lord of the Rings watch parties . . . four-hour extended versions only, of course. I would fight my way out of a sentient laser tag game with you guys any day.

To my agent, Tamar Rydzinski, thanks for having my back in every battleground, no matter how treacherous. You believed in *Team Chu and the Battle of Blackwood Arena* from the very first and never doubted that this book would find an amazing home. Thanks for everything you do! Thank you also to Ezra and Itiel for reading an early draft of the manuscript. If I owned a laser tag arena, you three would be on the leaderboard and guaranteed to get a lifetime of free games and snacks!

Trisha de Guzman, I knew you were "The One" for this book since our earliest phone calls. Your enthusiasm and intuitive connection to all the characters (but especially to Sadie!) have been invaluable, and this story is in the shape it is in because of you. Your genius "What if . . ." questions helped make the story even more intense and the game more exciting. Thank you for everything, and I hope one day soon we will finally get together for lunch!

Thank you to the whole team at FSG and Macmillan Children's, including Brittany Pearlman, Elysse Villalobos, Melissa Zar, Leigh Ann Higgins, Johanna Allen, Lauren Wengrovitz, and Megan McDonald, for welcoming *Team Chu and the Battle of Blackwood Arena* and me into your family with open arms, and for all of your hard work turning these pages into a real book. The videos Trisha sent me of some of you talking about the manuscript and sharing your personal experiences made me cry. Your imprint published some of my absolute favorite books growing up, and I am honored and grateful to now be one of your authors.

I'm lucky to have amazing friends I can call up to do battle with me in the arena at a moment's notice. But I want to thank two in particular: Melody Marshall, who has been a true-blue friend since almost the very beginning of this publishing journey. I always appreciate your notes and insight on my manuscripts, and our massive text chains about dogs, TV, and endless baking! And Naima Dennis: I'm so glad you agreed to be the COO of the Blackwood Gaming Arena. Our weekly three-hour Wine and Whines are a big part of how I got through the nightmare that was 2020, and I am so grateful for your friendship. Thanks for always listening, never judging, and crying as hard as I do at every movie we watch.

As always, I am endlessly grateful to the booksellers, librarians, and educators who get my books out to young readers. Everything you do is so appreciated, and I hope to thank many more of you in person someday soon!

Finally: I wrote this book for every Vietnamese American kid who rarely (maybe never!) sees book characters who look like them, eat the same foods they do, and have families like the ones they have. *Team Chu and the Battle of Blackwood Arena* is also for every kid who is obsessed with fantasy worlds, who dreams of growing up to tell stories, who has a sibling (or a friend or relative who's like a sibling!) they would both battle *and* go to battle with, or who has ever wanted to prove themselves. As Sadie's Bà ngoại tells her in the book: "You can do anything."

GOFISH

JULIE C. DAO

When did you realize you wanted to be a writer?
Very, very early on. I was always a big reader as a kid and I loved the idea of being an author myself. I wrote my first "novel" (twenty-five pages, handwritten, and illustrated!) when I was nine years old. And I've always kept diaries since then, too.

How did you celebrate publishing your first book?
By crying a lot and eating tons of cake! I worked so hard to get published and it was so much fun to call up friends and family to let them know it was finally going to happen.

Where do you write your books?
I usually write at my desk in my office, surrounded by books. Sometimes I write on the couch, but I tend to get sleepy there because it's so comfortable!

What challenges do you face in the writing process and how do you overcome them?

I love writing the first draft of a book, but I don't love doing the revisions! They can get really messy, and sometimes I have to delete entire chapters (or even characters) because they're just not working. As much as I don't like revising, though, I always roll up my sleeves and get really into the process because I know my book's going to be so much better when I'm done.

If you could live in any fictional world, what would it be?

I don't have a specific world I would want to live in, but I'd really love it if I could do magic and also travel through random household objects, like mirrors and wardrobes. It would save so much time!

Who is your favorite fictional character?

I've always liked Lyra from *The Golden Compass*. She's sassy, smart, and brave!

What was your favorite book when you were a kid? Do you have a favorite book now?

One of my favorite books was *A Rat's Tale* by Tor Seidler, about a young rat who loves painting and has to help save his rat community from humans! I bought it when I was nine or ten, and I still have the same copy sitting on my shelves today.

What's the best advice you have ever received about writing?

I think the best advice is to just sit down and finish the work. It's easy to come up with ideas and much, much harder to push through and actually write an entire book. It takes a lot of motivation and hard work, but you can't get published if you don't have a whole book first!

What do you want readers to remember about your books?

I want readers to feel like they get swept up in the action whenever they open up one of my books. My hope is that my stories will be exciting, magical, and adventurous. The best compliment is when someone tells me, "I totally lost track of time when I was reading your story!"

Don't miss another adventure with Team Chu!